The Test

The Test

John Reinhard Dizon

Chapter One

Katia Wynter woke up that morning with a terrible hangover.

It was the aftermath of yet another Friday all-nighter where the kids got together at Stewy McBride's barn, dancing to live music and drinking microbrews and moonshine. They partied the night away without a care in the world, and would probably do it again tonight before sleeping it off Sunday. Monday morning would begin another work week in TrC[1], and once again the kids would be reminded that they still depended on their parents' world for survival.

After the War on Terror and the rise to power of the New World Order, America was still in process of rebuilding its society along with the rest of the global community. Nuclear attacks had plunged the world economy into a Great Depression, and the government was doing all it could to keep Americans from starving to death. Food drops were being made on a monthly basis in cities across the country, just as the US had delivered food to starving nations over the past centuries. Families were disintegrating in record numbers as fathers abandoned their families to avoid watching them suffer. Teenagers drifted off to Sixties-type communes to live off the land and search for a better future outside the world their parents destroyed.

Katia lived in a tent on the edge of camp, having moved away from home against her parents' wishes. Her father, like most of the men in what was left of the city, was self-employed in the salvage industry. It was just another way of saying that he dug for recyclable items in the ruins of downtown TrC, selling waste by the pound for whatever the Government buyers would buy at the daily rates. She was sick of watching her Mom and Dad waste away, sharing their food with her while they grew skinnier each week. Besides, all the kids

---

1. Truth or Consequences

were moving away, and they were enjoying their freedom while coming into town to visit on weekends. Considering the thousands who had been killed or maimed by terrorist attacks, everyone was mostly glad just to be alive.

She knew her father was going scrounging this afternoon (he hated the term), so she would drop by about six PM with some baked bread and have some lentil soup with her parents. She knew her mother hated her being out of the house but was slowly getting used to it. She would stay overnight and come back Sunday evening before sundown so she wouldn't have to risk running across any Zodiacs. The rival biker gang from Elephant Butte would not risk a direct confrontation with the Excelsiors, but still roamed the night looking to steal, kill and destroy as the opportunity presented itself.

Katia felt very secure in knowing that Devin Kilrush had his eye on her. Devin was a year older than her at seventeen, and was the Vice-President of the Excelsior Motorcycle Club. It was well known that he and the club President, Mark Excelsior, were best friends, which placed the full might of the Club solidly behind him. He wasn't like the other bikers, though. He was shy and polite in a day and age when being a jerk was the coolest way to act. Yet you didn't mess with Devin, because that was like going up against Excelsior himself.

Part of her routine on Saturday mornings was taking a ride out to the Eastern Outland on her dirt bike to clear her head after Friday night partying. She was thrilled to see jackrabbits, birds, lizards and even snakes that had survived the nuclear blasts and the wind-driven radiation. It made her feel like there was hope for a new tomorrow, a chance that they could return to yesterday, back when everything was normal. No one wanted to live in the present, because the present was all about sickness and death.

There was an abandoned church about a mile away from the commune. There had been a work camp out there before the Terror Wars, and it was deserted after the terror gangs began setting up headquarters in the desert to conduct campaigns against the cities. They perfected the strategy in the Middle East and Africa, and it worked perfectly in the Southwest USA. It was said the US Army won the war but lost most of the battles. It didn't really matter anymore, the Wars had ruined everything. At least this little church was still standing. The little church had survived. It was like a monument to peace and love that Katia liked to come out and admire.

She thought she saw movement as her bike crunched across the glazed sand about a hundred yards from the Church, and it caused her to break out in a cold sweat. It could not have been Zodiacs because there were no bikes around, although the bikes might have been hidden around back. It may well have been a mirage, but it could be a fatal error to misjudge. Yet if it were survivors, it was everyone's patriotic duty to bring them back into society, or what was left of it. They could be treated for radiation sickness, given food and shelter, and help them re-enter what was left of the American community.

Radiation sickness had superseded genetic cancer as the number one killer in America. Cancer caused by radiation exposure exceeded all other forms of cancer by 500%, death rates in America had gone up proportionately, and infant mortality had reached 90%. Hospitals were overcrowded, most of the major insurance companies worldwide had gone bankrupt, and most people self-diagnosed with cancer simply stayed home and died. Alcoholism and drug abuse was rampant in a society wanting only to make the pain go away.

All these things were ricocheting around her head as she rolled the bike ever closer to the church. Once again she thought she discerned movement inside the church past the half-open front door. She froze in her tracks, listening intently for any sound, but all Katia could hear was the desert wind whistling through the cactus and the sagebrush. She felt like turning tail and going back to the commune for help, but then the outsiders might return to the desert where they would surely die. America had sworn itself to bring all its citizens back from the wastelands, and Katia believed in the Vow as she believed in her country itself.

"Hello?"

Katia was within twenty yards of the adobe church, rolling the bike up ever so slowly as she was able to see inside. Most of the tiles on the roof had been cracked or blown away, and most of the stained glass windows were broken. Yet the interior looked intact, the pews still in neat rows though the stone floors were covered with a thin layer of dust. She got off the bike and walked it closer, certain that if she grew frightened she could hop back on and zoom off. Devin himself had tuned this bike up, and he always kidded her about taking good care of her 'pocket rocket'.

She then heard it, the sound of one voice, then another. It was like the sound of two people being roused from sleep, and at once she was sure they had come here after traveling through the night. She would tell them about the commune, then go back and find a couple of Excelsiors to come back and get them.

"Hello, young lady."

She stared in wonderment at the bearded man who came to the door of the church. He was wearing a brown robe and sandals, his dark hair draping his shoulders. He gazed intently at her, as if staring into her soul though he was about twenty yards away. His blue eyes were as tanzanite, the African quartz that her father had given her on a necklace for her thirteenth birthday. Somehow she knew that fate had brought her to meet this man, but in this day and age, one could never be too careful.

"Hi," she said softly. "Are you from around here?"

"No," he managed a chuckle. "No, I'm afraid not. We took shelter here and spent the night. Are you the owner?"

"I told you this was a place of worship," a gruff voice called from inside the church. At once she recognized their Middle East accents and became afraid. She knew that if they were terrorists, she would not stand a chance. "Of course she doesn't own the place."

The speaker came to the door, a powerfully-built man clad identically to the first man, though his hair and stern eyes were dark brown. She saw two other figures staring through the window, and they came up behind the second man. All of them wore robes and sandals and were obviously unarmed without transportation.

"I am Paul," the blue-eyed man introduced himself. "This is Peter, and those are our friends, John and Simon. We have come a long way and thought we might stay here unless we are unwelcome."

"I'm Katia," she simpered. "Pleased to meet you all."

"Look!" the black-haired man named John spoke, spotting a jackrabbit crouching by a stand of cactus. "There is food!"

"What!" Katia exclaimed. "You can't eat that! You'll get sick and die!"

"Hah!" he scoffed. "And you think I care!"

At once he sprinted towards the cactus, and the jackrabbit streaked off as John began ripping the cactus apart with his bare hands. She was astonished as he picked the thorns off the cactus at lightning speed, peeling it and breaking it in chunks to hand out to his friends. She politely declined a piece, knowing the nasty-tasting pulp had been eaten by Indians centuries ago to avoid starvation in the wilderness. She knew she had to get them to the commune for something to eat.

"Say, look," she suggested, "let me go back to the commune and send some of the guys back here to give you all a ride. We can give you some food and water, and bring you into town where you can get yourselves situated."

"This is God's house, is it not?" Peter nodded towards the church.

"Well, yeah," she conceded.

"Then we shall stay here. We will fix it up, and welcome all those who come to worship," he decided.

"You can't stay here," she protested. "There's snakes and poisonous insects. Plus it gets over a hundred degrees out here."

"What is that?" John wondered.

"What, degrees?" she stared at him. "You're kidding."

"Please, John, we discussed this," Paul said gently. John raised a hand and walked over to where Simon had taken over the cactus-peeling.

"You can't stay out here, you're practically in the desert," she insisted. "Look, let me send a few of the guys out, you'll like them. They're real cool, I promise. I'll even come back with them, and once you feel comfortable, you can come back with us, okay?"

"Is this your transportation?" Paul walked over by the bike.

"Yeah, it's a Yamaha YZ450," she said proudly. "It's a titanium four-valve, it kicks when it has to."

"It doesn't seem practical," Peter muttered to Simon. "The chair seems comfortable, but seems a heavy object to bring along for a simple luxury."

"She was probably taking it elsewhere when she saw us. I'm sure it has other uses."

They sprung back into defensive postures as Katia got on the bike and gunned the engine, extolling its virtues to Paul before cutting it off as he seemed ill at ease with the noise.

"Not bad, eh?"

"Impressive," he replied.

"It'll take me about ten minutes to get back to the commune, and we'll be back in about a half hour. Will that work for you?"

"I believe we will go to the water instead," Peter decided. "There we will wash and catch fish and rest. We can refill our goatskins and return. We will meet you here at sundown and have dinner together. Your friends will also be welcome."

"Okay, wait," she held out her hand. "That's about five miles from here, and the sun's coming up. Plus you have no gear, and there are no rental places along the south stream. Please, trust me on this."

"We will meet you here at sundown," Paul assured her. She watched dumbfounded as they went back in and gathered their cloaks and goatskins. They were equally astonished as she hopped on her bike and zoomed back towards the commune.

Katia and three of her friends found the strangers along Elephant Butte Lake, which branched off into streams crossing throughout the wilderness. Katia was a lovely girl who stood 5'6" at 140 pounds, with a generous bosom and an hourglass figure. Her emerald eyes highlighted a lovely face, her golden locks swirling in the wind as the four bikes roared in to where the men reclined peacefully beneath a sycamore tree.

"Hey, guys," she said brightly. "These are my friends, Devin, Clyde and Homer. That's Paul, Peter, John and Simon."

The boys came forward and shook hands with the men. Devin noticed that Peter balked until given a look by Paul. Devin was immediately impressed by Peter's steely grip.

"Would you care for some fish?" Paul offered.

"Why, uh, sure…well, we'll take a bite," Devin hesitated. He was a tall, athletically-built teen with long blond hair and piercing blue eyes. "You sure got lucky. I don't remember the last time anyone caught any fish from this stream. I don't want us to eat up your catch."

"Why, no trouble at all," Paul insisted. "We invited Katia to bring you to visit us at the church where we are staying. We had not expected you out here. We've caught a few, and there's plenty more where they came from. We'll set some more on the fire."

The men invited the teens to sit with them on the grass. The teens accepted the fish bemusedly as Simon offered them skewed on a slender tree branch.

"Hey, this is great," Homer munched happily on the blackened fish. "Got anything to drink?"

"I believe there is more than enough," John nodded towards the lake.

"Are you nuts?" Clyde stared aghast. "You can't drink that water!"

"The fish came from the same water," Paul spoke up, cutting off John's retort.

"He's got a point," Devin looked hard at Clyde, then grew affable with Paul. "Where are you from?"

"We have come a long way," Paul furrowed his brow. "I come from a place called Tarsus. My friends here are from Galilee."

"Paul of Tarsus and..." Devin's eyes lit up. "Okay, right. Whatever. Were you out in the desert long?"

"Long enough," Paul replied mildly.

"What made you come out this way?" Homer wondered. "You could probably find work in TrC."

"Is Teer Cee the city to the north?" Simon motioned.

"We have no need of work," Peter reminded him. "We are here to save men."

"That explains it," Devin surmised. "That's what you were doing in the desert."

"Hey, dude, are those your bags?" Clyde motioned towards their pouches by the tree. "Didn't you bring any clothes with you?"

"We are dressed for the wilderness as you are dressed for the city," John munched on a chunk of striped bass.

"Well, guys, we can see about getting you some clothes from town. What sizes do you take?" Devin asked.

"I'm not sure," Paul shrugged as the others looked to him.

"I'm pretty sure they're all extra-large shirts, probably thirty/thirty-two pants," Katia decided. "They're okay with the sandals."

The boys took the men on the back of their bikes and brought them back to the church, then headed back to town with a couple of striped bass. Katia and Devin returned a couple of hours later with a couple of travel bags full of items.

Devin made them all agree to let him handle the situation with the men, and would explain it to Mark Excelsior. They figured the men were sent by the Government to urge any terrorists hiding in the desert to turn themselves in. They were probably Bedouins who would convince the terrorists that it was a genuine offer. They obviously lived in the desert so long that they knew nothing of modern conveniences. Paul appeared to be the leader but he and Peter seemed of equal rank. Devin would work to set up a sitdown between Peter, Paul and Mark Excelsior on Monday morning after the weekend's partying was over.

Katia and Devin had the bags strapped to their seats, and were thanked by the men as they saw it also included fruit, bread and cheese. There was also a book, and Paul seemed thunderstruck as he began leafing through it.

"What is it?" Peter asked, alarmed at the look on Paul's face as were they all.

"It—it's just a Bible," Katia was taken aback. "I thought you might want one since you wanted to stay here in the church. You guys aren't Muslims, are you?"

"This is Scripture," Paul managed. "It is intact, complete. This is impossible!"

"Let me see," Peter came over and attempted to take the book as John and Simon rushed over.

"Wait, Peter," he insisted, tugging it back. "There are chapters here in the back bearing my name. There are letters I've written. This is madness!"

"There's—more—Bibles—around somewhere," Katia wanted to make them stop quibbling, but she couldn't wrap her head around what they were saying.

"This is too weird," Devin stared uncomprehendingly. "I don't believe this stuff. These guys are on drugs or something."

"Maybe they got taken into some kind of experiment, a mind control project," Katia tried to compose herself. These were big guys, and if a fight broke out, she and Devin wouldn't be able to do a thing about it.

"I am Peter!" he shouted. "I demand to see this Book!"

"So be it," Paul handed it to him as he walked away towards the doorway, staring sightlessly out into the desert.

"What did you see?" John asked, looking back and forth from Paul to Peter.

"Your name is in there," Paul said hoarsely. "You wrote about the Christ."

"Peter, if you insist on keeping it to yourself, then I insist that you have the courtesy to read aloud," Simon demanded, then was suddenly rendered almost speechless. "Wait. Hold on. Where did you learn to read?"

"Why, I—!" Peter turned angrily, then stopped dead in his tracks.

"It is the Comforter," Paul turned, stroking his beard in contemplation. "It is as the Lord said. He is giving us powers and abilities in this age that we did not have before."

"Okay, what do you mean, in this age?" Devin squinted as Katia had to sit down on one of the dusty pews, her legs growing weak. "Where do you guys really come from?"

"It is as we said, we are not liars," John spoke out.

"Here," Peter gave the Bible back to Paul. "This is too much for me to absorb at once."

"You say there are more of these," Paul looked to Katia. "Can you bring them here?"

"Why, sure," she managed. "I'm sure there's quite a few around in town. We'll bring you a couple of boxes full."

"What do you mean?" Peter demanded. "How can there be so many available?"

"Don't," Devin held his hand up to Katia. "Don't go there."

"We'll ask people if they would be willing to donate them to the church," she replied.

"That seems good," Peter conceded.

"Where shall we put this Book?" John asked. "This place is covered with dust."

"Well, why don't you just keep it in your bag so it doesn't get—" Devin began.

"Keep the Word of God in a bag!" Peter was incredulous.

"Peter!" Paul admonished him. "These are Gentiles, and they mean no harm."

"Well, we *are* Christians," Katia said quietly.

"What!" Peter exclaimed before Paul came over to him and began speaking to him in hushed tones.

"Look, I brought a tablecloth for the altar in there, and candles," Katia revealed. "I'll get it cleaned off nice, and you can set it up there, okay?"

"I ask that you tell no one of what you have heard and seen here," John entreated the teens. We will assimilate into your society, it will take but a short time. I am sure we can help your people study and understand the Word, just as you can help us understand your culture. If there are those among you of like mind, bring them here tonight. The Sabbath begins at sundown, we can celebrate together."

"Are you guys Jews?" Katia blurted.

"We are—", John fumbled.

"Read the Book," Paul called over, his hand on Peter's shoulder. "Come tonight."

"What are we gonna do?" Katia wondered as they headed back to their bikes.

"Wing it," Devin gunned his engine. "Like they are."

The teens streaked back to the commune, wondering how on earth they were going to bring the two worlds together without a terrible collision.

Chapter Two

Katia returned that evening just before sundown along with Devin, Clyde and Homer. They had brought Mary and Martha along with them, two lovely young sisters who were struggling to fit in at the commune. They were not used to all the heavy partying, and were often chided by the others for not enjoying themselves on weekends. Clyde, however, had taken a liking to Mary, as Homer did towards Martha. The six of them looked forward to the diversion from the weekend ritual, and it had taken a great deal of discussion with Mark Excelsior to have gotten his well-wishing.

"Man, I don't like not having you around for the evening," Excelsior was upset when confronted with the news from Devin late that afternoon. "You're my party buddy, dude. Those other guys can't keep up. Ten beers and they're either passed out or acting stupid. I get sick and tired of having to babysit the whole crew after midnight."

"Well, maybe they should lighten up," Devin noted. "It's kinda dumb trying to keep up with Mark Excelsior. Anyone out here can figure that out."

"You do a pretty good job, brother," Mark patted his shoulder. Excelsior was a big strong kid at six foot and 210 pounds, a middle linebacker on the high school football team before the mini-nuke attack. It had wiped out City Hall in downtown TrC and leveled buildings along a ten-block radius, Truth or Consequences High School along with it. "Okay, if it's that important to you, go on and make the outsiders feel at home. Two things, though. I want to meet them, and we need to get them hooked up with the city folk in TrC. I don't want adults here in the commune, you know that. One thing leads to another, and pretty soon you have a committee trying to dissolve the commune and make everyone go back home. It took too much work to set this thing up, Devin. No adults, period."

When the teens arrived at the church, they parked their bikes and walked inside to where they saw the four men on their knees in prayer around the altar. Paul stood to greet them and motioned for them to take seats in the pews at the front of the church. They slipped into the pews and watched as Simon stood and gave them tiny cups of wine and pieces of bread on a small wooden platter. They were all familiar with the ritual from their youth, wondering where the men got the bread and wine from.

"Blessed are you, Lord our God, Master of the Universe, who has given to us holidays, customs and seasons of happiness, for the glory of the Lord Jesus the Christ, the Light of the world," Paul held the bread and wine aloft. "Here is the body and blood of the Christ. We do this in commemoration of His sacrifice for all men so that sins may be forgiven."

The teens consumed the bread and wine, surprised that the ritual was being done at the beginning of the service rather than the end like everyone else did. Yet they considered the fact that they were some kind of Bedouin Jewish Christians, so probably did things differently than everyone else. Possibly they didn't know what they were doing.

"I brought the Bibles I told you about," Katia offered after they had prayed. "I put them in a box and wrapped them in a nice blanket. I'll bring them in if you like."

"Please do, my dear," Paul was grateful. Katia rushed out to get the box along with a sackful of goods for the men. Devin introduced the men to Mary and Martha in the meantime. The sisters had honey-blonde hair, hazel eyes and shapely figures, and were very well-mannered. Katia placed the sack in the rear pew while bringing the boxful of Bibles up to the front.

"How can this be?" Peter marveled as she produced twenty Bibles of different colors and sizes.

"They must have a way of mass-producing these books," Paul replied. "Just as armies hasten production of materials in time of war, they reproduce these books in times of peace."

"That seems right and just," John nodded.

"Wait until somebody takes them on a tour of the *Herald*," Clyde muttered to Devin. "Talk about culture shock."

"Shut up," Devin hissed.

Paul next distributed the Bibles and they all took a seat as he read Chapter 53 from the Book of Isaiah. The teens were impressed by the reverent tone he used in reading the text, a far cry from that they had grown used to at the churches of their childhood.

"Let us share from the word of God," Paul said as he concluded the passage. "What questions have you about the ways of the Lord?"

"Well..." Clyde tried to measure his words, "why does God allow things like the Terror War destroy our lives? If He is all good, then why does He allow evil to get over? How can Christians say He is all-powerful if the Devil always wins?"

"The War has not destroyed your lives, it has merely made room for all the new things that must come into your life," Paul said gently. "If you move into an old house, sometimes you can replace things and make the house like new. If the foundation is solid and the framework is strong, you can simply restore the rest. Sometimes the house is not worth saving and is cleared away to make room for a new and lasting home."

"Evil never wins," John pointed out. "Evil forces us to make choices, and when we make the right choice we are the victors. When we choose poorly, evil remains to test us again. However, the tests never end. It is just as it is at your schools. God continually tests us so we can continue to advance. Alas, only some of us go on to greater tests. Many repeatedly fail and become trapped by the evil because they do not believe."

"Consider the man of violence who becomes proud and full of himself and his might," Peter spoke softly, which greatly impressed the teens. "He will take his army out into greater and more dangerous battles, because evil is all-consuming and knows no bounds. The rich man, the lustful man, the glutton is insatiable, their greed knows no end. So it is with the man of violence. Although his skills increase and he becomes greater and more powerful, he leads his men into greater slaughter until one day he meets his match and is annihilated. From there, the new warlord goes forth and does the Devil's work. Yet the Christians endure to pray for the souls of the lost, that they may put down their weapons and seek God."

The teens sat in wonderment as the words of the men made them reconsider many things that were on their minds. It was difficult for them to set aside their disappointment and bitterness towards the religion of their parents. They had seen too much hypocrisy, too many inconsistencies, too much alienation and strife between the churches and the community, much less between the congregations themselves. Yet these men were different. They looked like the kind of men who would look very comfortable on a motorbike, yet there was a holiness about them that was almost intimidating.

"We normally conclude our meetings with a hymn," Paul explained, "but I am afraid you may not know the words or melodies we sing. Is there a song of yours we can share?"

"Oh, wow," Katia murmured. "How about 'Amazing Grace'? Everyone knows that."

"How is that sung?" Simon asked.

"Well, let's see if I can remember," she said. "I'll write the words down on this notebook in big letters and put in down on the altar so everyone can see it. We can gather around the altar and sing."

"Excellent idea," Paul grinned.

> Amazing grace! How sweet the sound
> That saved a wretch like me
> I once was lost, but now I'm found
> Was blind, but now I see
> 'Twas grace that taught my heart to fear
> And grace my fears relieved
> How precious did that grace appear
> The hour I first believed.
> When we've been dead ten thousand years
> Bright shining as the sun
> We've no less days to sing God's praise
> Than when we've first begun.

"That is a wonderful song!" Paul marveled after they sang it twice. "I thank you so much for sharing it with us."

"It is one that the heart can dwell on," Simon admitted, humming it softly to himself. The teens grew strangely silent, many of them trying to clear their throats and fight back tears of nostalgia. It brought back feelings that made them feel terribly uncomfortable.

"Well, we better go," Katia wiped her eyes. "I know you all will be having Church tomorrow."

"Tomorrow?" Peter wondered. "The Sabbath begins on Friday at sundown. The sun sets at the end of the Sabbath on Saturday."

"You mean you guys are tied up here from Friday night to Saturday night?" Homer marveled. "That's gotta be some hardcore religion!"

"You better chill out, mister," Martha nudged him.

"He's just saying that most of the folks around here go to church on Sunday," Devin glared at Homer.

"That should be no problem," Paul decided. "We will simply have meetings all weekend. We will accommodate all those who choose to make merry and indulge themselves at night. We will show them that there are other ways to expend their energies. Tell your friends that there will indeed be church here on Sunday."

"I think some of the girls might be interested in coming up here," Mary ventured. 'Lots of them are a little homesick, but they don't like going home to visit because they always end up fighting with their parents. They can't go to church either because the people in the congregation are always trying to give them a lecture and tell them to do what *they* think they should do. It's just a real hard time for everyone right now."

"You seem unhappy," Peter asked Clyde. "Is something wrong? Do we offend you?"

"No, heck no," Clyde mumbled. "It's just my tooth's been hurting. I usually have a few drinks around this time and it makes it feel better, that's all. I like you fellows, I like it fine here."

"Let me see," Peter stood before him.

"What? I ain't gonna—" Clyde objected.

"Let him see," Devin growled at him. Clyde reluctantly opened his mouth and Peter looked inside, then stepped back and waved his hand before his nose.

"Rotten," he winced.

"Very diplomatic," Paul rolled his eyes.

"Happy?" Clyde snapped at Devin.

"Well, are you two performing a Greek comedy or are you going to help him?" John demanded.

"Why don't you give him a lecture about patience being a virtue?" Peter asked Paul, then turned to Clyde. "All right, boy, let's get on with it. Do you believe in the Christ who is your Savior and died for your sins?"

"Why, uh, yeah, I guess," Clyde managed.

"Don't be a jerk, Clyde," Devin growled.

"Yeah," Clyde admitted. "Yeah, I do."

"Blessed are they who know the name of the Lord and are saved," Peter grabbed Clyde by the jaw and the back of his neck. "In the name of the Lord Jesus Christ, you are healed!"

He released Clyde, who fell backwards and lay sprawled on the stone floor.

"What—?" Katia gasped as the teens looked upon him in astonishment.

"He is fine," Peter grunted. "He is praising God. Are there any others among you who are suffering from afflictions?"

"No, no," they all held up their hands. "We're fine."

At length Clyde began to stir, and rose to a sitting position.

"My—my toothache," his eyes widened. "It's gone!"

"Hold on there," Homer gave him a hand and pulled him to his feet. "Open your hole, lemme see."

"I just thought he wasn't into toothpaste," Mary said to Katia.

"Holy—!" Homer exclaimed before Devin came over and blocked his mouth with his hand. He pulled away and announced, "He got brand new teeth! Brand new teeth!"

The other teens rushed over to see, and took turns looking into Clyde's mouth until he finally shoved free.

"What am I, a horse or something?" he wiped his mouth.

"Can I get new teeth?" Martha asked Peter. "I got a crooked one on the side."

"Nay, you are beautiful just the way God has made you," Peter touched her face affectionately. "The crooked tooth serves to remind you of your imperfection when you look down on another girl who is not as pretty as you."

"Tell no one of this," Paul instructed Clyde and the others. "We have not come here to entertain or to draw attention to ourselves. We have come here to make men think and to draw them close to God."

"Women too, right?" Katia asserted.

"Women are a part of men, child," Paul insisted. "A man's most perfect part."

"I don't know how people get the impression you don't like women," Simon was quizzical. "Maybe it's those letters you wrote. Maybe you might've phrased them better."

"It is as Pilate once said," Paul frowned. "What I have written, I have written."

"Be that as it may," Peter cocked an eyebrow. "I suspect there are so many copies of the Holy Book around by now, there is naught to be done about it."

"Okay, Clyde, you heard what the man said, mum's the word," Devin said. "Say, guys, I guess we'd better be getting along now. We'll spread the news and see if anyone wants to come up here tomorrow morning."

"I'm sure they will," Katia gushed, and hugged Paul tightly around the neck. He hugged her back, and soon they were all exchanging embraces. The teens had not had close contact with parental figures for so long that it nearly brought them to tears. The men could sense the strong emotion welling within the teens and were deeply touched as well.

Katia showed them the sacks at the rear of the church before they departed. The men thanked them for the bread and cheese, yet were bemused by the pants and shirts she had brought.

"The upper garments are attractive, yet somewhat constricting," Peter said as he tightened his belt before pulling his arms loose from his robe to try on a shirt. The teens marveled at the musculature of his torso, reminding them of a pro athlete back when sports were all the rage.

"I fear your vanity might get the best of you should you change your style," Paul noted wryly as he saw the admiring glances of the girls. "You had best remain as you are."

"And thus does the pot call the kettle black," Peter retorted. "The Great Apostle."

"Your opinion is appreciated as always," Paul was sardonic.

"I bet you'd look great in a black shirt," Martha smiled at John.

"I bet you had best be on your way home," John grinned back.

"He's right," Homer tugged on a belt loop on her jeans. "Let's go."

The teens got back on their bikes and roared off back towards town as the men waved goodbye behind them.

"So, did you have a good time down on your hands and knees with the holy rollers?"

"Don't hack on them, Mark, they're cool people. I say we let 'em alone, they can't do no harm," Devin insisted.

The teens returned to the commune where the Saturday night party was going full blast. A bonfire had been ignited at the Excelsiors' clubhouse, which was an abandoned barn that the gang had restored. They had painted it black with silver trim, and a large pentagram had recently been painted over the entrance. The club's colors were black and silver, and their leather vest uniform was decorated by a ram's head in the center of a zodiac wheel. Mark had adopted a demonic theme in order to enhance the threatening aura of the gang.

"You're right," Mark walked over to a stand where one of the gang mamas was handing out cups of microbrew. He took a couple, handing one to Devin. "Once the kids see through them, they'll be rejected just like the parents, and they'll have no place to go but north. We'll just let them blow off steam, and then they'll blow away. It's great I got you around to cool me off. If it was just me, I'd ride on up there and burn the place down."

"Maybe them being out here will have a good effect on some of the kids," Devin considered. "They've got a good attitude, they're not pushy. They don't try and make people see things their way. If the kids get homesick, they may just start going out there to talk to them instead of breaking camp and running home. They're having church tomorrow morning, I think we should spread the word and let the kids take advantage of it."

"Hey, back up a bit," Mark downed his cup in one gulp as Devin sipped his beer. "I don't want this thing to turn into a fad and have everybody skipping Party Night like *some* people I know. Let it just go word of mouth and we'll see what happens."

"Okay, fine," Devin allowed. He looked out at the makeshift stage set on an area about fifty yards from the barn where a death metal band was performing. The gang had set up a generator that provided power for the bands, and over a dozen groups had joined the club just to have a place to play. They were considered the road dogs, a level below the bikers on the upper echelon. The mamas and the go-fers were the third rank, and those considered the lowest were those in the commune who were not part of the gang. Mary and Martha were among the few. Devin was not good with the way things were, but he was not about to have a falling out with his best friend over that which would not change.

"Say, I think we're ready to set up that crib in Devil's Holler," Devin changed the subject.

"Yeah? How so?"

"I told you we've been moving stuff down there, and I've been sending our best taggers and sidewalk artists to chill the place out," Mark revealed. "They been bringing me camera shots, and I think we're gonna give it a go on the first Friday of the full moon at midnight. Now ain't that gonna be something."

"Man, I think we're going somewhere we may not wanna go," Devin disagreed. "I was good with the whole idea of all that supernatural stuff scaring people, especially the Zodiacs. You know what's gonna happen, though. They ripped their name off the symbols on our colors. Next they're gonna start ripping off all this demonic stuff just to try and keep up with us. I think it's gonna be a whole lot of bad karma going around. We can be big and bad without going around playing like devil worshippers."

"Oh, what's the matter, little Devin afraid of ghosts?" Mark teased him.

"C'mon, don't get stupid," Devin winced. "Had too much to drink already?"

"What are those, chicken feathers?" Mark brushed Devin's buzzcut with his fingers. Devin smacked Mark's cup out of his hand, and Mark tackled his legs and dropped him to the ground. Devin did a sit-out and went for a leglock as Mark tied up one of his arms in a chicken wing. They meshed together into a pretzel and strained against each other until, after about five minutes, they rolled away from each other and lay panting on the ground.

"That lead singer from that new band, the Warlocks, man, she is hot, dude," Mark folded his arms under his head as they gazed at the stars. "I think I'm gonna check her out."

"Yeah, well, don't push too hard and run them off," Devin drew his legs up. "They're a great band, they got some great chops."

"Looks like you're doing okay with Katia, huh?" Mark looked over at him. "If I get hooked up with that Delilah chick, maybe we can go take a ride somewhere. How about the beach, dude? I was thinking of the Gulf Coast."

"Half of it's radioactive, and the other half's oil spill," Devin said wryly. "You know the terrorists knocked the heck out of that area."

"Yeah, maybe we can just stay here. I was thinking about clearing the Zodiacs off the lake anyway. Once they're gone, we'll have the whole lake to ourselves."

"C'mon, Mark. If we go to war again the City said they'd call in the National Guard. If they move in here they'll put the whole area under lockdown. They'll bring a bulldozer in here and it'll all be over. I'm not worried about us, but all the kids in the commune'll have no choice but to go back home."

"Including Katia?"

"Yeah, genius, including Katia."

"Well, don't worry about it. If I get Devil's Holler fixed up the way I want it, we can move the whole commune up there and the National Guard's trucks won't be able to make it out there. Plus they'll think we cut and ran, and they wouldn't waste the gas to send choppers out to look for us. Besides, I'm not gonna take the Zodiacs out until the time is right. We'll go in at night, one big move, and take them out in one shot. I'll let you know when I've got it set up."

"Just think about it before you make your mind up," Devin insisted. "The Zodiacs are no threat to us. We don't need another war, or any heat from the law. Go on and do whatever you're gonna do with that Devil's Holler of yours instead."

"So you gonna go down with me and check it out?"

"Yeah, yeah, I'll check it out."

"Good," Mark rolled up to a sitting position and slapped Devin on the thigh before hopping to his feet. "Let's go get a beer."

"Okay," Devin took his hand and pulled himself to his feet. They sauntered back to the party area where dozens of teens were drinking and dancing, tossing all their cares aside for the evening. They had come to find peace at the commune, and hoped that they had left the turmoil of their parents' world behind once and forever.

Devin only hoped he could continue to calm the storm that was Mark Excelsior.

Chapter Three

The teens took the two-mile hike from the commune to the church the next morning before sunrise so as not to have to walk in the heat of the desert sun. They had made arrangements to have the bikers bring them back after the service, at which time they would have sufficiently recuperated from last night's hangovers. There were twelve of them in all, ten girls and two boys, all of whom came from middle-class homes and were not used to the heavy partying that the bikers encouraged.

It was Mark Excelsior's intent to turn the commune into a city within a city, an alternative existing side-by-side with their parents' world. Excelsior was an intelligent boy who maintained straight A's in order to remain captain of the football team. He had carefully thought out his plan for the future and had discussed it at length with Devin and the other gang leaders. The commune would be as a malignant cell that would feed off TrC until the mother city expired and only the commune remained. Most of the inhabitants of TrC had migrated to nearby Albuquerque to take advantage of more available government benefits. It was slowly becoming a ghost town that had dwindled to about two thousand residents. The young people continued coming out to the commune, and there were about a hundred teens living in tents out in the desert.

Excelsior knew that time was on his side. Once the town dwindled down to the 1,500 mark, it would be easier for his men to begin pilfering twice as much home improvement material than they were now. They would also be able to haul some sheds, storage huts and even trailers out here. They would grow bigger as TrC kept shrinking. Once South TrC was abandoned, it would be time for the Excelsiors to make serious plans to take over the town.

Only they were experiencing their own leakage problems as the straight-edge kids were seeking their own alternatives. They took comfort in the protection of the biker gang, yet the partying and the violent atmosphere troubled their spirits. They only hoped that something else would materialize out here in the desert, a place where they could live in relative peace and harmony. When Katia told them of the strangers at the church, they grabbed the opportunity like drowning persons clutching at flotsam.

As the sun rose over the desert around seven AM, the teens found that the men were taking full advantage of the abandoned equipment inside the church. They had found folding tables and chairs which they set up at the rear of the building, and it almost looked as if they were getting ready for an outdoor sale. Only they were at work cleaning the equipment with water they had toted in plastic jugs from the lake. It was obvious to Katia that they had been up most of the night getting set for the morning service.

"Welcome, children," Paul was jovial though his face was strained from lack of sleep, as were they all. "How wonderful that you have all shown up. Come inside, make yourselves comfortable and we will begin our worship."

Katia introduced the men to the teens, and they were all delighted to meet one another. The teens occupied the front row seats as Paul stood at the altar, the other three men seated off to his right. They had passed out Bibles so that everyone could follow along as Paul read from Chapter Thirteen of the Book of First Corinthians.

The teens were spellbound as Paul read the words as if they were his last. The truth of the statements seemed to jump out at them as a living thing. They all had their own idea what love was about. Yet they had been proven wrong and disappointed so many times throughout their lives that it seemed almost as an abstract concept. They had read the Bible a few times over their lifetimes but they didn't remember anything as intense as this.

"And now these three remain: faith, hope and love. But the greatest of these is love," Paul concluded, staring past the teens out the open church door, almost lost in his own thought.

"You wrote that?" Peter muttered, and was lightly elbowed by John. The teens caught the exchange and felt glad to have been privy to the inside joke. It was like an icebreaker, seeing that the men were not as stern and humorless as those in their parents' churches.

"The *writer*," Paul gave Peter a withering glance, "had sent this as part of a letter to friends in a distant land where they had built a church, not much different than this one. When the rabbi—the teacher—left the town, his fellow believers got distracted and were led astray from the path they had chosen. The teacher was very disappointed and poured his heart out in a letter that he sent to his friends in that town. Apparently his words took effect on some, and they resolved themselves to eventually get the church back on track."

"So it is with this church," Peter rose from his seat and came to the railing along the dais where the altar was situated. "Leadership does not come from within, but from Christ who rules on high. You must simply open your hearts, and the Spirit will speak through you at the appointed time."

"Aren't—haven't you guys come here to stay?" Katia asked plaintively. "At least for a little while?"

"Yes," Paul assured her. "For a little while, at least."

"What questions do you have about the letter?" John got up and came over, sitting on the altar rail. Once again the teens were impressed by the informality of the meeting.

"Is it wrong to kiss boys and hold hands?" one of the girls asked shyly.

"It is not so much what you intend, but the impression that you make on others," Simon came forth to the surprise of his friends. "Suppose I went into Teer Cee and set up a fruit stand or, even better, a fish stand? Of course everyone would come around to see what I have to offer, as fish appears to be a commodity in these parts. If I were to set some fish aside and people were to come and inspect it, soon they would assume that this was my intent if I did nothing to discourage them. If they came up to me and asked if they could have some of the fish, and I agreed, it would encourage others to ask for fish. Yet, if others watched from a distance and saw people taking fish from the stand, they might assume that they could simply walk up and take fish without even bothering to ask."

"I think I see where you're coming from," the girl pondered his words.

"Moreover, consider the man who pampers his dog and allows it to lie on his bed, and even take scraps from the table. In the middle of a feast with his friends, imagine the dog jumping up and snatching the main course from the platter on the table," Peter elaborated. "Should the man beat the dog for its ignorance or hold himself to blame?"

"How should we get over broken relationships?" another girl asked, her thoughts nearly bringing her to tears. "Sometimes it seems like the more you pray, the less God listens."

"Never think that, child," Peter came around the rail and walked over to the girl, brushing a tear from her cheek. "Never. Just because God does not answer right away doesn't mean He is not listening. This is why it is important for us to study the Scripture. Every answer from God can be found therein. Often He allows us to work things out ourselves because we already know the answer, but refuse to accept it. We continue to question until we receive the answer we want, not the answer that comes from God. When you search your heart, my dear, you may find that this is where God has left the answer."

"Sir, why does God let so many people get killed?" another girl was saddened to the point of distraction. "Why do so many good people die? Why do little kids die before they get a chance to see what life is all about?"

"Suppose I was able to take your hand and take you to another place?" Simon came over and held her hand in his. "Imagine a place where there was no more sorrow, no more tears, where the streets were paved with gold and angels sang and praised God on every street corner? Think of a place where every man and woman owned their own mansion, made especially for them, with everything they ever wanted inside. Imagine wanting to go on a trip and see something new, and being able to simply take off and travel through the stars? Could you imagine being in such a place for a day, a week, even a whole month?"

"It would be wonderful," the girl wiped her eyes. "You're talking about heaven."

"Moreover, imagine being reunited with all those who have gone before you. Can you think of one who has died that makes you think of these things?"

"I lost—my whole family," she began to weep.

"Imagine being back together with them in this wonderful place, forever and ever, to never be split apart ever again," Simon continued. "Now in the midst of this joy, let us suppose that the prayers of your friends were answered, and the angels informed you that you would have to leave. You would indeed be separated from your parents and your family again, and returned to this world to be put to the test once more. Would you not think your friends inconsiderate?"

"God wouldn't do that," the girl insisted. "He wouldn't make someone leave Heaven."

"Exactly, my child," Simon patted her cheek before returning behind the altar rail.

"Let us sing a hymn and go outside to have breakfast," Paul suggested.

"How about 'Amazing Grace'?" Peter suggested. "I greatly enjoyed that song."

"Now is a perfect time to strike the Excelsiors," Hakeem Mogambo suggested as he paced the adobe shack along the eastern outskirts of Truth Or Consequences near Elephant Butte Lake. "The fools are lying around hung over after their drunken rows last night. If we cruise out there and seek our opportunity, we can possibly toss some cocktails[1] and create havoc in their camp before they can respond."

"And do what?" demanded Jhonny Rodz, the president of the Zodiac Motorcycle Club. "Give them a reason to come out here and firebomb our commune? You know we can't match them with force, they have more bikes and better fighters. They know it and we know it, and if we move against them again they'll press the advantage. We have to catch them at a worse disadvantage than having hangovers. Those dogs live with hangovers, it's not going to keep them from coming out to fight."

"We're losing face the longer we sit on the sidelines and let the Excelsiors strut their stuff along South TrC!" Hector Alindato, the Zodiac warlord, fumed. "More and more kids are moving to his commune while people keep moving out of the South Side. Don't you think he's going to plan on moving in and taking over some of those abandoned buildings? He'll start getting more and more refugees while we're stuck in gear with the National Guard patrolling the East Side facing our territory. If we don't even the field soon, he'll get too strong for us to mess with. Now or never time is coming, Jhonny."

"I think our best option is to make people think twice about moving into his commune," the Zodiacs' Councilor, Mahmud Shabazz, postulated. "If we make some moves in town to make some of his people want to move back, then it not only decreases his numbers but makes him look weak. Everyone will realize that his gang can't be everywhere at once, and they'll see that his influence is limited."

"So who do we hit, Mahmud?" Jhonny demanded. "Who can we hit and not have to worry about them hitting us right back?"

---

1 Molotov

"The families, brother, the families!" Hector's eyes lit up. "If we drive out and hit the families when they're out getting supplies or scavenging, they'll beg their sons to come back home to help protect their property. That'll weaken the Excelsiors or at least cause problems with the club members. It's better than just sitting on our hands while they're getting stronger."

"It's risky, bros," Jhonny stroked his bearded chin. "The last time we went up against them they sent ten of our guys to the hospital. I know six of theirs went too, but that seriously cut into our manpower and resources, having to go out and get medical supplies and care for our wounded. All right, Hakeem, I'm giving this to you and Hector. You plan it out and run it by me before you go out. Take four of our best guys with you, and don't you dare mess this up. If the Excelsiors take us to war, somebody's gonna answer for it."

"Don't worry, boss man," Hector grinned. "The Zodiacs strike silent, quick and hard, like scorpions in the sand, brother. Like scorpions in the *sand*!"

Hector touched fists with the others as was their custom, and together with Hakeem they went out to finalize their plans.

The church picnic was a festive occasion, with the teens slowly bonding with the men as the hours passed on. The teens told them all about the effect of the Terror War on TrC, and the men gained tremendous insight on the city and its society and culture in the process. Each of them had their own horror story to tell, and it was cathartic for them as they shared their pain with one another.

"These stories are common to those who have endured war," Paul said quietly after the teens had shared their tales. "Unfortunately it is the innocent who suffer the most during these times. The men of war have strengthened their resolve, they have assessed the risks well before they put their plans into effect and brace themselves for the outcome. Yet, as it is written, those who live by the sword will die by the sword. Blessed are the peacemakers, for they are the sons—and daughters—of God."

"Glad you threw that in there," Peter grunted.

"Your people will have to rebuild," Simon told them. "As you know, we too have come from a turbulent region of the world. Our people have endured persecution throughout the centuries, yet we have endured, and so will yours. It is only through faith and devotion to God that we persevere, and so shall yours. Yet, as it is written, the child shall lead the way, and so it must be here. Your parents have suffered great setbacks, and they will question themselves and their ways. They may lose faith in God, and it is by your example they will regain it."

"How can we help them regain their faith?" one girl wondered.

"You are here," Peter smiled. "This is where it starts."

"These Bibles," Paul came over to Katia as John prepared the last of the fish. They only brought back as much as they needed so that nothing went to waste in the desert sun. "Are there more of these around?"

"Yes," she was hesitant. "To tell the truth, there's a stack of them at the thrift shop. Lots of people lost their faith after the bombings. It's not like they actually turned their back on God, but they lost their faith in the Bible. There's this big thing about the end of the book, the Revelation. They said that those who believed were supposed to be taken away when this happened. They were supposed to have been brought up to heaven. They weren't supposed to have gone through this."

"This is not the end, my dear," Paul encouraged her. "This is merely a time of testing. This is why we are here, to help you endure the test for the tribulation to come. You see, just when mankind has reached its limits, when they feel they can endure no more, the Evil One will take advantage of their loss of faith. He will say, 'Where is your God? He has turned His back on you'. He will offer his own solutions in exchange for people's trust, and trust is faith. Men will no longer seek peace and happiness, but will return evil for evil. In that day, the end times will begin."

"How much time is left?" Katia was alarmed.

"God will give you all the time He thinks is necessary."

"Now that stuff is starting to come back to me, little by little," she touched her fingers to her temples. "My parents used to take me to Bible School when I was small. They used to read all the old stories, about Adam and Eve, Cain and Abel, Noah and the Ark, Samson and Delilah, all that stuff. They were like fairy tales, they were stories that gave a message, like Aesop's Fables. But the back of the Book, the New Testament, that was the real thing that told the future. There was this—guy named Paul—" her voice faltered.

"Never think of those stories as wives' tales, Katia," Paul said softly but firmly. "Do you believe that the Bible is the Word of God?"

"Well, yes, but wasn't the Bible written by men?" she asked tentatively. "It's been interpreted so many times and in different ways, how do we know what is right?"

"In here, my dear," Paul touched his chest. "In your heart. This is where the Holy Ghost resides within you. He came to dwell as far back as you can remember. The heathen call it conscience, but I assure you it is the Holy Ghost. When a small child breaks something, or creates a mess, or harms a smaller creature, it experiences turmoil in its soul. It looks to the parent for guidance, and it is then when it first learns what is considered right and wrong."

"That kinda makes sense," she mused.

"Even if the parent spoils the child, the Holy Ghost will continue to tug at its heartstrings," he continued. "When the child goes out into the world, it will see the difference between their relationships and those of others, and will seek out the authority of others for guidance. The Holy Ghost inspires this. However, if the child continues to reject these things, eventually the Comforter is unable to provide solace for the troubled spirit. And so it is with the Scripture. If a person rejects the Word of God, they close the doors of their heart so that even the Spirit of God cannot enter."

"I see," she tried to absorb it all.

"The Word of God is a collection of letters dictated by the Holy Ghost," Paul explained. "Only the Law of Moses was written by the hand of God, and the lack of faith of the Hebrews caused Moses such rage that he destroyed the very tablets they were written on. It shows us how even the most precious things in this life can be shattered in just one moment of anger. But the Holy Ghost continued to inspire men to write on His behalf, and His words have endured for over six thousand years. The Devil has tried to dilute this Word, he has tried to add to and subtract from them, but God Almighty cannot be thwarted or subdued. The Bible as preserved by the ancients is one. It is without flaw or contradiction. Why did Jesus call Himself the Word? It is simple, dear. It is because He is the embodiment of the Word, and the Word is God. If Christ is not perfect, the Scripture is not perfect, and the reverse is true."

"It's so hard to defend it all," she recalled. "People who don't believe come up with all these arguments, and ask all these questions, and sometimes they make you feel so foolish. When you're the only one in a group of people, they can make you feel so alone in your beliefs."

"This is because you were a child with a child's knowledge," he reassured her. "When people ask a young child why something is so, they reply, 'Well, because my Father said so,' and that is as it should be. When the child gets older, they begin to understand the ways of the Father and they can explain why the Father says it is so."

"You make it sound so simple," she said softly.

"That is because the Holy Ghost is the Teacher, and He makes it simple. Just start reading your Bible again and you will see. He will teach you."

"Hey, come on and get some fish before it runs out," Martha came over to them. "It's just wonderful. I can't remember the last time I had fresh fish. Everybody said all the fish in the lake were dead."

"Paul?" Katia called as he followed Martha back to the campfire.

"Yes, my dear?"

"You've been giving out bread to everyone, and you had wine for communion last night. Almost no one has bread and wine. Where'd you get it?"

"A man came out of the wilderness, and he had a sack of loaves and a goatskin of wine," he replied. "He only asked for our blessings in return, then he returned to the desert."

"Where did he come from?" she insisted.

"Who can say?" Paul smiled mysteriously.

"Did he come from where you came from?" she managed. "Where *did* you come from?"

Paul waved his hand and returned to the campfire.

Chapter Four

"Do you think they'll like me?"

"They're gonna love you, are you kidding me?"

Katia and Devin gunned their engines that Monday morning just after dawn, planning to cruise up to TrC to visit his parents before his Dad headed off to work. The Kilrushes lived in a one-story frame two-bedroom home on East Sixth Street, not far from where Devin had gone to school. Sierra Elementary School had since closed, its students merging with those at TrC Elementary after the terror bombings. Devin had gone on to Hot Springs High School where he had played football alongside Mark Excelsior before the terror attacks.

The teens were alarmed by the sight of police cars having converged along the intersection of Sixth and Kruger Street. Devin's heart pounded as emergency vehicles had surrounded the Kilrush home. The police saw he was wearing the Excelsiors' colors, which he wore to deter anyone from messing with him and Katia, and prevented him from approaching the house. Yet one of the officers recognized Devin from his football days and waved him in.

Katia was shocked that such a thing could be happening. They had talked about her going with him to meet his parents, and four weeks ago it was just something he had brought up in conversation. Two weeks ago they had made out for the first time, and though she would not let him fondle her, it was as if the relationship had become serious. Last week he made it sound as if it was really important to him, and she agreed that they should go. She had thought of numerous scenarios, but not this.

Devin saw his parents out front speaking to investigators, and he rushed over to exchange hugs and find out what had happened. Katia approached timidly and stood near the bushes where the walkway met the sidewalk along the front lawn. The police were exchanging notes and paid little mind to her as they saw her arrive with Devin. She could see there had been a fire out back of the house, and it looked as if a storage building had been burned out. His father was being strong but he had a grave look on his face as Mrs. Kilrush was entirely distraught.

"We smelled smoke, it was about one in the morning," she could hear Mr. Kilrush telling his aggrieved son. "I got up and saw there was a fire in the shed out back. Your Mom tried to run out in the yard because the dogs were locked up in there. We started leaving them back there at night because of all the robberies in the area after the bombings. By the time I got out there it was too late, the fire must've gotten to some of that painting material I had out there. It just went up in a ball of flame."

"Eddie and Schultz and Lucky were all back there," his mother sobbed.

"All three of them?" Devin's voice grew hoarse. "Why?"

"You know how they were," she cried. "If you put one, he'd think he was being punished. If you kept one inside, the other two'd think you were favoring the other. They'd bark and cry all night."

"We heard motorcycles going up and down the street after dark last night, and we were hoping it was you and your friends," Mr. Kilrush said. "After a while, we just didn't pay no mind. It's always been quiet around here, even after the bombings. We weren't expecting any trouble, especially anything like this."

"Is that your friend?" Mrs. Kilrush motioned towards Katia. "Go ahead and invite her in, I'll get her something to drink. Come on, bring her inside."

Devin took her hand and followed his parents into the house. Like everywhere else, it seemed smaller than he remembered. The feeling was enhanced by living in the great outdoors for such a long time.

"My name's George, this is my wife Jimmie," Mr. Kilrush introduced them.

"I'm Katia. Devin's told me so much about you both. It's wonderful to meet you."

"I just wish all this wasn't going on," George lowered his eyes as the Fire Department vehicles prepared to leave outside.

"Excuse me," a police sergeant rapped softly at the threshold as the door had been left ajar. "Devin, can I have a word?"

"Sure," Devin allowed.

"I'll go with you, son," George offered.

"No, stay here with Mom and Katia. I'll be right back."

Sgt. Bill Clemens was a stocky, bull-necked man who had backed down biker gangs and closed down drug dealers throughout a twenty-year career with the TCPD. Only the terror bombings had become a force beyond his control, and he felt increasingly useless as his beloved community unraveled before his eyes. This attack by local biker gangs was something he was used to dealing with.

"I want you to let your friends know I'll be taking care of this," Clemens insisted. "We don't need any more trouble out here like we had a couple of months back."

"Look, you're calling me aside like I'm somebody special, and something's gonna happen because of it," Devin was upset. "Now if I was so special, you think this would've happened in the first place?"

"I think this happened just because you're special," Clemens squinted. "Maybe you boys figure those colors are some kind of warning sign you wear for everyone to see. It also works the other way around. There are other fellows like yourselves who may just as well see them as targets on your back. Everybody knows you're one of the ringleaders of that gang of yours. They wouldn't have made a stupid move like this if they didn't have something up their sleeve. You let me look around and I'll handle this the right way."

"How are you gonna do that? My parents were asleep when they torched our shed and killed our dogs. I know how the game works. If you got no witnesses you can't do anything. You know who did it; the only other biker club in this area is the Zodiacs. I don't know how much you know about the rules of the road, but you don't go out hurting civilians over club business."

"That's right, they broke the rules of T or C, and I'm gonna make 'em pay for it, not you or Mark Excelsior," the sergeant was adamant. "I didn't ask you out here to ask for your help. I'm telling you to tell your gang to stay outta my way."

"That's fine, Sergeant," Devin turned and headed back inside. "I appreciate anything you can do to fix our shed and get our dogs back."

The four men at the Church heard the familiar roar of motorbikes in the distance, and gathered as the dust clouds eventually gave way to the four figures approaching. Yet the riders were unfamiliar as they cut off their engines and sauntered up to where the men stood.

"Morning, gentlemen," the leader spoke up. "I heard all about you fellows and thought I'd come on out to introduce myself, get to know you guys. I'm Mark Excelsior, and these are my partners: Skull, Cueball and Pipeline."

"I am Paul, and this is Peter, John and Simon. Won't you come inside and have coffee?"

"Much obliged, friend, but we're good. I just wanted to come out and see what you had going out here. Those kids who came out here yesterday went back to the commune talking about how great you guys were and the wonderful things you were talking about. Why, they've got twice as many kids coming out this Wednesday, from what I'm hearing. Now, some of these kids won't give us the time of day. I just can't help but wonder what it is that's getting you guys over with them."

"We preach a sermon of love," Paul explained. "We speak of peace, love and joy. From what they tell us, this has become hard to find in their city."

"Well, now, have you been to TrC?" Mark wondered. "Do you know for sure that's true? There's more than a few places like this in town, and lots of them closed down because they run out of things to sell. Matter of fact, there's Bibles everywhere. People are just giving them away."

His three friends sniggered, staring cockily at the four men.

"When we get around to visiting your town, perhaps some of your Churches will be reopened," Paul ventured. "Just like this one."

"Peace, love and joy," Mark reflected. "You know, my grandparents moved out here back in the day talking about those things. They were hippies, you know, moving out here to the desert to meditate and become one with nature. As it turned out, all they got to become one with were snakes and scorpions. My parents had dreams of leaving here and having a better life somewhere else, but then I came along and messed that up for them. Now, I grew up on the straight and narrow, and became the All-Star quarterback here in New Mexico. Everybody loved Mark Excelsior. Everybody but the terrorists, that is. When they blew up the town, then nobody cared about Mark anymore. No one cared about anything but saving their own skins. All that peace, love and joy stuff went up in them mushroom clouds. Fellows, you're selling yesterday's news, and I'd hate to see you putting those old ideas back in those kids' heads when they came out here to find out what truth is all about."

"You are a foolish boy," Peter thundered. "You are like so many others who have come out to the wilderness to explore their own depths and coming up with nothing but evil. There can be no peace, love or joy without the God of Light. If you continue to seek the Prince of Darkness, he will shield you from the light and control your life to steal, kill and destroy all you hold dear!"

"Wow," Mark arched his eyebrows, standing with arms akimbo. "That's some heavy stuff. You know, that's what my grandparents ran away from, all those big city Bible thumpers having that big escape clause: the Devil made me do it. You live like hell six days a week, then pray it all away on the seventh. You make up a boogeyman, then all you got to do is blame everything on him when things go wrong. Problem is, it wasn't no boogeyman that blew TrC to hell, now was it?"

"So why do you go to that cavern to glorify the boogeyman?" John asked quietly.

"Oh, so now you been spying on us," Mark chortled. "They told me you went all the way out to Elephant Butte to go fishing, and I said that was a bunch of crap. Plus, if you came through that wasteland to get here, you fellows must get around in the heat on your feet real good. Okay, so you went out and saw us in the Holler. Just because we got it looking all spooky out there doesn't mean we're worshipping the Devil."

"The pentagram is a Mesopotamian symbol glorifying the gods among the stars: Venus, Jupiter, Mercury, Mars and Saturn. Venus is the apex point, symbolizing the Queen of Heaven, a direct challenge to the Almighty Father," Simon pointed out.

"So you guys don't like women," the bullet-headed Cueball sniggered.

"There go those rumors again," Peter murmured to Paul.

"Some of the most important figures in my ministry are women," Paul retorted. "This is nonsense. You are sidestepping the issue. If you glorify evil, you become enemies of Christ. You are forcing the children to make a terrible choice, and if you do so, you at least have the responsibility to let them hear both sides of the argument."

"You're taking a whole lot for granted here, preacher man," the heavily-tattooed Skull sneered belligerently.

"I think it's the other way around," Mark shot back. "Why do you think that, of all those who perished, you and yours were allowed to live by He Who has authority over life and death? Do you dare challenge He Who spared your very life?"

"Let me tell you something, holy roller," the mohawked Pipeline pointed at him. "You know, we had all these churches up and running in TrC back before the bombings. They had their services on Sunday morning, picnics on Sunday afternoon, prayer meetings on Sunday and Wednesday nights, youth activities on Friday night, why, just about everything you could think of. Well, when those bombs exploded and this town got blown apart, who do you think were the first ones to leave? They jumped outta here like rats off a ship and made tracks all the way to Albuquerque. You see, we already watched what happens when the going gets tough for Christians. When it's all sunshine and smiles, you people are on top of the world. When the chips are down, you talk about a God who just doesn't seem to care one way or the other."

"I'll let you in on something," Peter boomed. "This man Paul has taken more stripes in the name of Christ than you have pimples on your body, yet he's still standing tall. I've been arrested and spent more time in prison than you've had in school. Sure, your town's had its hard times, but it's always darkest before the dawn. The people of New Mexico are being sorely tested, and we're here to make sure they pass the test!"

"Hey, guys, this is all good," Mark stepped up to restrain his buddies. "You know, we've had a few whiners in our camp who don't care for our lifestyle and are looking for something a little quieter. I think I'm gonna have a little meeting at the commune and see who might be happier coming out here to stay. Now, of course, you fellows are gonna be out here on your own. If the Zodiacs come out here looking to kick some butt, you won't be able to come crying to me. You might be able to go running to the Sheriff in TrC, but I'm pretty sure you'd be better off praying for fire to come down from the sky."

"That can be arranged," John muttered.

"We accept your offer," Paul decided. "Hold your meeting, and ask those who will stand with Christ to pull up stakes and pitch their tents here among us. For those who would camp in the shadow of your Devil's Holler, our offer remains should any change their minds."

"That's a one-way road on from our end," Cueball snarled as the four bikers walked off. "Anyone who comes out here aren't gonna be welcome back with us. Make no mistake about it."

"I'm not ready to make that choice," Devin admitted to Katia as they discussed Mark's proposition later that evening. They had left the Kilrush home before sunset and returned in time for Mark's bonfire meeting. Katia and Devin, like the others, were taken aback by the either/or option, and no one made a commitment before the meeting ended. The couple took a ride out to the stream babbling along the commune along the southeast, and sat on the rocks mulling over what was said.

"I can't imagine what could have happened to cause Mark to come off like that," Katia shook her head. "That must have been some kind of argument they had at the church."

"I can't walk away from the Excelsiors before this thing with the Zodiacs is settled," Devin shook his head. "If you and I were to leave the camp, especially us, Mark would never get over it. He has too much pride. He'd see it as me turning his back on him, no matter how I explain it. Even if the Zodiacs came out and burned the church down, he would never let any of us back in. Besides, the Zodiacs got payback coming. Maybe after that happens, we can leave the Club behind us, but not just yet."

"Devin, don't you—hasn't anything that the men have been saying made any sense to you?" Katia was hesitant.

"What do you mean, all that peace and love stuff?" Devin seemed a bit testy. "The way I see it, it's like that old book, *War and Peace*. I'm all for love and peace, that's how my parents raised me up. This was like nirvana for my parents when they moved here to New Mexico from California. My Mom was able to open up her curio shop, my Dad was able to make a living as a carpenter, it was everything they ever dreamed of. When I came along and did well in school, started playing football, they couldn't have been happier. As it turned out, that's exactly what it was. We were all living in a dream world. No one ever dreamed those terrorists would set off a mini-nuke in New Mexico, let alone TrC. They burst our bubble in one day, shattered my parents' dreams of a lifetime in one bomb blast. Maybe it'll be peaceful again one day. Maybe you and me can start planning a future. But not just yet."

"I—I don't know what to say. I didn't know you felt that way."

"What, about you? Or about Mark turning his back on that church?"

"Both," she said quietly. "I care a lot about you too, and I don't want this to come between us. I'm hoping we can do the right thing together."

"You're not thinking about leaving the commune, are you?"

"I'm—I'm afraid of the men," Katia replied. "Not like I'm scared of them, not that way. I'm just afraid of that message they're sending out. You know, it's just like Mark said, all the Church people from TrC took off down the road to Albuquerque and left the rest of us hanging. Now Paul and his friends are here, and they're making it sound like God's giving us new hope. What happens if Mark convinces everyone to turn their backs on the men? What happens if they give up and go away? I think we'd lose too much if we let them walk out of our lives."

"So what are you saying?"

"I know Mary and Martha are probably going to leave, and maybe some of the other girls. I think I should go with them and make sure they're okay. Mark can't stop us from seeing each other—that is, if you still want to see me."

"You heard what I said. I want to plan my future with you. If you need to join Paul and his friends, that's fine. I just need to settle the score with the Zodiacs. My father's heart was in that tool shed. They took away his life's ambition when they burned it down. Those dogs—I raised them all when they were pups. They didn't deserve to die, not like that. You want to go on ahead, that's fine, but I got to do what I gotta do."

"Okay, Devin," she came over to him and kissed him softly on the lips. "You do what you think is best, and I'll be waiting for you."

Devin hugged her lovingly before they got back on their bikes and returned to the commune. Not only would he still have Mark behind him when he went against the Zodiacs, but he still had the Club at his back if he had to go out to the Church to protect Katia. He felt secure in having his feet in both camps, and knew he would be able to work it out before leaving the Excelsiors in his own good time.

Little did he realize that he would have to choose sides far sooner than he ever could expect.

Chapter Five

At the break of dawn that next day, Mark Excelsior and Devin Kilrush were surrounded by members of their biker club as they watched the great exodus begin. It was like the end of a huge outdoor music festival, as dozens of kids were taking down their tents and packing their gear. They spoke quietly amongst themselves, sharing drinks and packaged foodstuffs as they prepared for their mile-long journey to the little church along the desert.

"There's some good-looking women walking out of this camp," Brute shook his head as he watched the first few campers pulling on their backpacks and balancing their truss rods for the long hike. "We should've tried to keep them around for a while longer."

"For what?" Mark squinted at him. "We gave everyone a choice, and they made their decisions. Haven't you had enough rejection in your life? They clearly decided they want no part of us. I told them what would happen if they broke camp, and they chose to run off anyway. What do you think's gonna happen when they run out of food up there? Do you think those holy rollers will be able to bring back enough fish every day to feed those losers? Sure, they may be able to go into TrC and get provisions from the Government, but how long do think that'll last? They'll come crawling back here, you mark my words."

"You gonna take 'em back?" Cueball lit a clove cigarette.

"It depends what they're willing to do to get back in," Mark smirked. "Those sissy boys are gonna have to do some serious groveling, you can bet on that. By the time they're finished hauling and fetching whatever we say, they'll wish they never even laid eyes on a Bible."

"I'd let my imagination run wild over what we can ask them girls to do," Brute chuckled.

"Katia's leaving, Dev," Cueball mentioned. "Aren't you gonna stop her?"

"We spent a lot of time talking last night," Devin said tersely, giving the impression that he would not want to belabor the topic. "She's doing what she thinks is right. I asked her to stay but I wouldn't stand in her way. Nobody tried to make us stay in TrC, so why should we stop those kids from walking off? We'd be worse than our parents if we did."

"All right, this is over and done with," Mark exhaled tautly. "We got new business to attend to. We need to settle accounts with the Zodiacs for what they did to Devin's parents."

"I say we knock them down to size," Brute snarled. "I say we go in and take out their commune. They hit Devin's house, we hit all their living spaces. Fifty kids walk out of our camp, we run all their campers out of theirs. Maybe we've been weakened, but we need to make them crawl."

"That sounds like a plan," Cueball nodded. "We ride in there in the middle of the night with some flares and a few rifles, and they won't know what hit 'em. We set up some snipers out in the desert outside the camp, and they can pick off the Zodiacs if they try to come after us. There's no way in hell they'll be able to put out the fire in the middle of the night with all that desert wind blowing through. By the time the sun comes up, their whole commune'll be nothing but burned canvas. We can hit that dilapidated barn of theirs on the way out, and even their club won't have a place to lay their heads."

"If anyone gets shot, you know the cops'll be all over the place," Mark frowned. "They're gonna be expecting us to come out looking for payback for what happened to Devin's Mom and Dad. If we go in and torch the Zodiacs, this'll be the first place they'll come looking."

"Maybe we can use the holy rollers as an alibi," Brute had a flash of inspiration. "If we say we were out that way, the rollers'll have to give us up for the cops to be able to come down on us. We win either way, Mark. Either the rollers'll stand up for us, or they'll rat us out and the kids'll see that they're nothing but snitches. I don't care how much they're against our lifestyle. The kids'll know that if the rollers cooperate with the authorities, they'd give them up next just as soon as their parents start pressuring the City to bring the kids back."

"You may have a point," Mark decided. "I want the three of you to get together with Skull and put together a game plan. We'll have a meeting tonight and finalize everything."

"I appreciate what you're doing for me, Mark," Devin allowed as Brute and Cueball went off to find Skull. "We just need to keep things in perspective. They killed my dogs, and that hurts like hell. Burned 'em alive, and I'll never forget that. Still, dogs are dogs, they're not people. I can't—*we* can't—go in there and kill anyone for killing my dogs."

"We never planned to kill anyone, not before, not now," Mark insisted as they walked back towards the barn. "Those Zodiacs that got killed last time were casualties of war, you know that. You were in the middle of it, you know what it was like that night. Guys were swinging baseball bats, chains, lead pipes, chucking bricks at each other, it was hell on wheels. We didn't think Gizmo was gonna make it. If it wasn't for Katia and the girls watching over him, he'd like to have died. If we go up there and the Zodiacs come out to face us, I'm not leaving any of my boys out on the field. I bring all our guys back, whatever the cost."

"All right," Mark relented. "But no snipers. We can't set men up in the hills and have them picking people off if things get out of hand."

"C'mon, man, get real. The Zodiacs already told us that the next time, we'd better bring guns. If they come out on that field to meet us, there's a good chance they're gonna be packing. I don't want a shootout any more than the next guy. I just don't want us to be clay pigeons riding off if they come out firing on us. If we got snipers shooting back, they can lay down cover fire long enough for us to get away."

"I want revenge, Mark, you know I want revenge. I just don't want anyone to get killed. They burned my Dad's workshop, all his tools, and they killed my dogs. I want payback, but I don't want anyone to get killed. Okay?"

"Okay," Mark relented. "I just don't want you getting soft on me out there. There's no one in this club I trust more than you. There's no one in the world I want at my back when stuff hits the fan. I just don't want to have to worry that you're gonna hesitate long enough for someone to put a knife in my back."

"You know that could never happen."

"There's a first time for everything."

"Don't lay that line on me. I just let my girlfriend walk away from me so I could stick it out here with you."

"What happens after we settle your score for you? You gonna walk away then?"

"What re *you* gonna do, Mark?" Devin turned to face him as they stood outside the barn. "You can't stay here forever either. You know that eventually the National Guard's gonna bring everybody in. It's just like what happened in New Orleans after Hurricane Katrina. Once the government gets strong again, they'll start trying to control everything like they always do. They'll tear down this camp, and it'll be TrC or the desert. You can't stay outside forever."

"Maybe we'll go join the holy rollers," Mark patted him on the back as they went inside. "God always provides. Isn't that what they been preaching?"

The men at the Church came out to meet Katia as she rode out to meet them that morning. They watched as the slow procession of campers began arriving soon afterward. They carried their backpacks, tent materials and sacks filled with gear across the desert land. They were met by the men, who helped them pick spots to pitch their tents anew. They tried to have the newcomers set up close to the trees growing here and there. Soon there were no shaded areas available, and the rest had to camp out in the open alongside others.

"Now I know what Moses had to deal with," Peter shook his head as Paul walked about giving help and encouragement where necessary. "I believe that fellow Mark had the last laugh. He must have sent half his camp out here. We'll have to be replicating that miracle of loaves and fishes every morning to deal with this."

"Katia informed me that the children chose to come out here," Paul explained. "This proves that most of them were with the bikers for lack of a better place to go. We must rekindle their love for the Word in their hearts. Afterwards, all that will remain is to win the hearts of the bikers, then reach out to the people of Teer Cee."

"Ha!" Peter folded his arms. "That is a rowdy bunch that will be slow to learn. I fear the words of your epistles will fall upon deaf ears."

"Perhaps the Lord Jesus sent you and Simon the Zealot along specifically to reach that sort," Paul shrugged. "You should have little trouble reaching out to those of like mind."

"In that case, I see why you were sent, tentmaker," Peter retorted as he walked off. "Most of those shelters look as if they were put up by the children's grandmothers. As a matter of fact, I believe the grandmothers would have done a far better job."

"It looks like most of the kids found places to pitch their tents," Katia walked over as Paul prepared to fetch tools from the Church storeroom. "We had a wooded area down by the biker camp that gave us some shade during the day. I guess we'll have to make do out here."

"I'm pretty sure that the children will find plenty of shade by the lake," he assured her. "Peter goes out there every day, and he will be glad to take all those who want to provide for their own meals. I'm sure most of the children will be accompanying him."

"How are they gonna catch fish without any gear?"

"There is no difference from one desert to the next, my dear. Peter will show them how to fashion strips from the bulrushes in order to make fishing lines, and twist thorns into fishing hooks. If they are so fortunate as to catch a large fish, they can use their shirts to help capture them. Peter has fished all his life, there is no trick he is unaware of."

"I—don't understand how you're able to catch so many fish. The Government told us all the fish were killed by the mini-nukes, and that the water wasn't safe to drink. How are you able to do this?"

"Can't you see, Katia?" Paul said gently. "God is in absolute control. If He created the lake, and all the fish therein, do you think that man is so powerful that he can poison the water that he had no part in creating? If a child could destroy things in a home that a parent had no hope of replacing, would it not give the child power over the parent?"

"You make it sound so simple, as if God was just a phone call away," she shook her head. "How can you be so sure He's listening or doing anything? Can you hear Him talk to you?"

"Suppose you were an infant, and you were unable to leave your cradle to see if your milk was being prepared. Do you think your father would be any less receptive to your cries? Do you not think he would be even more concerned in watching over to you, knowing that you did not realize he was right there for you? Of course, once you learn to communicate, he knows that you can call to him at any time. Still, he continues to watch over you and all in his household nonetheless."

"It's just so hard to absorb. You make it seem so easy."

"This is because our belief is so strong, and that is because we have all seen the Lord Jesus. You have not, but one day you will."

"When I die?"

"Perhaps not. He can appear to you in dreams. It will not be in a dream as one who appears in a drama. Rather, you will know your Master's voice, just as the animals on the farm know the voice of he who feeds them."

"Can you ask Him to visit me in a dream?"

"You must ask Him yourself, He's your father just as He is mine. He will not appear in response to a challenge or a threat. His power is too great to deal in trifles. You must realize He can see inside your heart. When you call to Him with a pure heart, seeking Him as a child seeks their father, He will come to you. I guarantee it."

"It's kinda scary, isn't it?" she faltered.

"This is the first step towards God. Can you imagine when Moses encountered the burning bush, a tree engulfed by flames though not one leaf was even singed. I knew one man who was confronted by God while traveling on the road. God's power was such that the man lost his vision for three days. He thought he knew everything about God, but he soon found he knew nothing at all."

"It was you, wasn't it?" there was something familiar about the anecdote.

"Perhaps. It could have happened to one man, or it could have happened to many. Who can say? What's most important is how He appears to you. You must first approach Him with fear, for He is God. When He responds, He will speak with love and you will know His voice. From then on, you will know He will never leave or forsake you."

"I'm going to go looking for Him, and I know I'll find Him."

"I know you will too."

Out at the new campsite, the boys gathered around John and Simon as they visited here and there, ready to give advice or help as needed. Others crowded around Peter as he prepared to head out to the lake to go fishing.

"You'll need to wear loose clothing, and bring tools to cut firewood and make your fishing gear," he instructed them. "You'll also want to bring water jugs so you can bring some back here."

"We can probably get some gear from our parents, or at the thrift shops at T-C," one boy pointed out. "We might even be able to get rafts or canoes so that we can go out on the lake."

"As you wish," Pater replied, hoisting his sack onto his shoulder. "God will send the fish wherever He chooses."

"If the cops see so many people out fishing, they're probably going to be asking for fishing licenses again," another boy mentioned. "Maybe we should start applying for them."

"Render unto Caesar's what is Caesar's," Peter began walking towards the lake as everyone began to follow. "Just be certain to return the things of God to God."

"What things are they?" some asked.

"You'll figure it out."

The commune on the east side of Elephant Butte Lake was about seven miles away from Truth or Consequences, a short distance from Interstate 25. It was considered part of Elephant Butte State Park, impounded by the Elephant Butte Dam which created the largest man-made lake in New Mexico. There were US Coast Guard bases in the area which served as a reminder that the military remained active in the area. The National Guard often used them as rendezvous points when patrolling the vicinity. There had been a strong military presence around the State Park after the terror bombings, but after most people had evacuated north to Albuquerque, the National Guard had gone northward as well.

The Elephant Butte commune, or EBC, was more sophisticated than the Excelsior commune. A group of hippies living outside of Albuquerque decided to join the group after the bombings. They reasoned that the EBC had a better chance of survival since they were located closer to the reservoir and were further away from both TrC and Albuquerque than most. That would provide for less Government interference and restrictions that might be mandated. They brought their experience to EBC, and the group proved far more self-sufficient as time passed.

They helped the group modify generators that powered a double-wide trailer home serving as the commune's administration center. They next encouraged the Zodiacs to bring as many car and golf cart batteries as could be scavenged from TrC. They used them to rig up 12-volt trickle charge systems, recharging the batteries to be used in the tents and cattle trailers where the EBC members resided. The kids were able to use them to hang Christmas tree lights and small devices that could be powered by cigarette lighter charges. Kerosene lamps and portable outhouses abounded, and voluntary units provided services as required.

The EBC had its own carpentry and electrical crew, a farming and composting group, as well as a bakery, a firewood and recycling team, and an alternative energy club. Plans were being made to begin research on steam-powered units, which was greatly favored by steampunk enthusiasts. The EBC relied on the Zodiacs for scavenging in exchange for marijuana which they grew in hidden gardens outside the campgrounds.

There had been no security measures to alert the commune when the motorcycles were walked up to its perimeter about three o'clock that morning. The Excelsiors had cut off their motors about two hundred yards from the EBC to keep the noise from carrying across the countryside. Mark had mustered his fifty hardcore members to take part in the attack, and they were well armed for the occasion. Ten of them had brought hunting rifles and would take positions around the camp should the Zodiacs respond with gunfire, or if an Excelsior biker's life was in danger.

Mark had the group split up so that Devin led his men to the east and Mark to the west in order to bracket the commune. He left ten men at the south entranceway to the commune, ordering them to spread out in protecting the flank of the first strike team. They, in turn, prepared to follow the second team into action on a signal from Mark. He circled the camp until he could see Devin's group in the shadows, walking their bikes along the eastern perimeter. He flashed his headlight at Mark, who flashed him twice in response. It indicated that the trap was set.

At once, Mark and his nine bikers gunned their engines and switched on their headlights, as did Devin and his group. Each biker had a sackful of flares attached to his handlebars, and they began igniting the flares and tossing them onto the roofs of tents and storehouses. They also threw them into every open doorway they could find. The commune erupted into chaos as the residents rushed into the open, trying to make sense of what was transpiring. They were shocked at the thought that the Zodiacs had suddenly turned against them. Only some recognized the colors of the Excelsior bikers, and the word spread that it was their neighbors who were trying to destroy the camp.

First the children, then the women roll out of their sleeping bags and watch the mad parade. It is a theatre of madness, the biker orchestra playing a concerto of chaos. The air is filled with thousands of fireflies, hot ashes swirling frantically around the camp, blown to and fro by the desert wind. There is a cacophony of roaring engines, as the war cries of the bikers echo alongside those of weeping girls and sobbing children. Now and again there is a muffled crash as a storehouse collapses or is shoved down by one of the bikers.

Now and again a girl rushes up to a biker, begging and pleading him to convince the others to stop. For some reason he thinks it an opportune time for romance, to engage in conversation. Some of the more exuberant ones try and pull the girls to them, to seat them on the back of their bikes and whisk them away. The girls scream and cry even louder, and at once there is Mark Excelsior who cruises by and orders his cohort to desist. Destroying homes, wrecking property and setting everything in sight ablaze is the order of the day. This is no time for courtship. They all have a job to do.

The battle cry is Devinshome, a mythical place that was destroyed by the Zodiacs not long ago in a land far, far away. As the girls plead and cry, they begin to understand that Devinshome is actually in TrC and that it was attacked just days ago. They try to explain that they are not part of the Zodiacs, never have been, never will be. They start to realize that most of the bikers don't care. They are here exercising themselves, letting off steam, having a good time. This beats lying around a barn, drinking beer and listening to death metal. That kind of activity is okay for relaxation. This, *even* this, is what they joined the gang for. Even though they claim to be doing it for Devinshome, they are really doing it for themselves.

The little kids fantasized that their Dads might be riding in on motorbikes to save them, to beat up the bad guys. Even though many of them left for Albuquerque after the bombings, or even long before that, there was always a chance. Their Dads were the biggest, strongest and toughest guys on the block. They would teach these bullies a lesson. They would punch these Excelsior guys right in the nose for burning everybody's tents down.

At once a hue and cry went up as a distant storm of bike engines grew ever louder. The girls and the children began yelling and cheering at the sound of the Zodiacs coming to the rescue. All the young men who had run out to fight off the Excelsiors had their faces smashed, their heads split open, their arms cracked. They were lying in the mud alongside the broken jugs, the charred tent posts and the torn clothing. The Zodiacs would avenge the insult. They were more than equal to this task. Like the Excelsiors, this is what they lived for.

Only the Excelsiors did not come to fight, they came to destroy, they came to avenge Devinshome. They disappeared as suddenly as they arrived, the roars of their departure stereophonic with those of the Zodiacs racing on the scene. The Zodiacs knew they had come too late, and cursed and swore how they would avenge the loss. The boys and girls did not care. They just wanted things to be the way they were a half hour ago. They wanted things to be the way they were before, back before the strangers came into their world months ago and blew it all away.

They wanted to be back in a place called home.

Chapter Six

News of the attack on the EBC spread throughout TrC as the blaze had alerted police cars patrolling the lake area. Fire trucks and ambulances came out but the residents of the commune insisted on cleaning up their own mess. Family and friends of those who were at the Excelsior commune were concerned that the altercation may have impacted their loved ones, and drove out to inquire. They learned that many of the teens had relocated to the Church property, and headed north to find them.

Over two dozen parents drove up in a small convoy. Upon parking and exiting their vehicles, they felt a strange sense of calm the area had not known since the bombings. Whenever they had visited the Excelsior commune, the teens seemed to be constantly bored, in want of something to do. Here they were engaged in menial chores, arranging the grounds by their tents or working inside the church. At length Simon came out to meet the parents.

"Welcome to the church," he greeted them. "We've only been here a few days, but many of the children have come out to pitch their tents alongside us. We have welcomed them with open arms, just as we welcome you."

"What kind of church is this?" the crowd asked. "Are you Protestants?"

"We are Christians," Simon squinted. "We serve the Lord Jesus Christ."

"Do you lay hands, that kind of stuff?"

"We do whatever the Lord commands."

"Who's paying for all this?"

"The Lord provides. Go, then, the children can direct you to your loved ones. They can answer all your questions and enjoy the day with you."

"Say, buddy, my name's John Pinkston, I'm a reporter with the *Sierra County Sentinel*. Mind if I ask you a few questions?"

"I am Simon. I have been known as the Zealot."

"Yeah, and why's that?" the fat man waddled alongside Simon as they walked towards a stand the kids had set up for the collection of firewood.

"At one time I belonged to a group that was devoted to the physical salvation of Israel. I know now that the true battle is a spiritual one."

"Yeah, well, with the trouble they're having over there with the Arabs, I don't know if they're there just yet. So what's with this commune you got going out here? The only ones that have been able to make it have been the Excelsiors and the EBC, and they're both protected by biker gangs. How are you able to take care of these kids out here?"

"We take care of no one. The Lord God provides for us all. We have met with the Excelsior boys just as we meet with you. Should the Zodiacs come here, they are welcome too."

"Those boys you're referring to just trashed the EBC last night. I don't think if the Zodiacs come out here they'll be looking to pass a peace pipe around."

"The Spirit indicated there had been a disturbance. We were told to wait and offer counsel as best we can."

"So, this Spirit," Pinkston scribbled notes on a small pad. "Is it like the Indians have, the Great Spirit? Or is it like some kind of Obi-Wan Kenobi thing, the power of the Force?"

"There is but One God. We are here to show this to you."

They watched as a police officer was led by Katia to where they were standing. Pinkston recognized him as Sgt. Bill Clemens.

"Excuse me, fellow," Clemens looked to Simon, then glanced at Pinkston. "Can I have a word?"

"I'll go on over and have a word with your partners," Pinkston nodded as he headed over to the church. Katia remained in case Simon needed any clarification She was fairly certain he still didn't have a clue about many things.

"Are you men renting this place?" Clemens asked.

"We found it to be a house of prayer, and it has been vacated. We have restored it so it can be used by others."

"I hear tell that you and those three friends of yours are staying here, is that right?"

"It suits our purpose for the time being."

"Well, I'll tell you, you're good for now. Since the bombings, the City's been pretty good about letting displaced persons stay wherever they can find shelter, provided it's not a hazardous structure. This place seems to be shored up pretty well. Once everything gets back to normal, there may be issues about property rights, taxes and all, but all that doesn't concern the TCPD."

"We plan only on completing the task given to us, and then we will be on our way."

"Where are you going?" Katia asked plaintively. "You wouldn't just leave us."

"We have come to reconcile you to one another, and then to God. There were just four of you who came out at first, now there are fifty. Once God has eased the pain in your hearts, you will be ready to return home."

"How can we go home?" she insisted.

"It's pretty bad back in TrC right now," Clemens admitted. "Have you been there?"

"No, but we intend to go into the city and visit the parents soon. Our mission is not to bring families together, but to overcome the forces of evil. Only when evil is vanquished can love and peace return to your city and your homes."

"You may want to keep your eyes open for the Zodiacs," Clemens told Katia. "If you've got any cell phones up here and you can get a signal, just call 911."

"Are people getting signals in town yet?"

"It's kinda touch and go. The Government says the radioactivity in the air may be blocking the waves, but some communications are getting through. We're seeing transmissions from the Emergency Broadcast System from time to time. Some of the local and public broadcast stations are coming through as well. It'll take time, but we'll get there. Well, you folks be careful, and call if you have to."

"Are you really going to visit our parents?" Katia asked as the police car drove off.

"You came out to live among the bikers because you trusted them more than your parents. You then came here to place your trust in us. Now we must convince you and your parents to trust in God. From His Word you will all know what is best for you."

"The church people left town, Simon. They betrayed the trust of lots of people. I don't know if all this religious talk's gonna go over too big."

"Don't you know that is why we were sent, child? The evil was too great for those before us to overcome. We have been sent to overcome the evil so that the Word of God may prevail."

"I guess so," Katia lowered her eyes. "I just hope you visit my parents last."

"Why is that, child?"

"My Dad's in construction, and his crew was doing work in the downtown area when the explosion went off. He had to pick up material outside of town, and everyone else was injured or killed. He was all messed up over it, and when he went to the local church for counseling, he found out they left town. I guess he ended up blaming God for everything."

"That is common. I will look forward to helping him reason everything out."

"Well, I don't know. He's really bitter and depressed right now. He and my Mom are always fighting. That's the reason I moved out, I just couldn't take it anymore."

"Everything works for the glory of God," he patted her shoulder reassuringly. "You'll see, things will be just fine."

Sgt. Clemens drove west along the country road and spotted the patrol car sitting outside the deserted McBride property that Stewy had supposedly left to Mark Excelsior for safekeeping. There was no way of getting in touch with Stewy and his wife. Rumor had it that they were part of the exodus to Albuquerque. The house was locked up tight and nothing had been changed outside of the barn painted black. Excelsior's parents had moved to California and had lost contact with their son. The police had little choice but to take Mark's word for it.

"Looks like the whole bunch of them just pulled up stakes," Officer Rochefort shrugged as Clemens came over to meet him. "All the tents are gone and the barn looks pretty empty. We thought we'd come check these guys out, and it looks like they disappeared."

Rochefort was part of the newly-formed Anti-Gang Enforcement Unit that was monitoring the numerous groups sighted around TrC. He had vainly sought to accumulate evidence against the Excelsiors over the attack on the EBC. The Zodiacs, like all other biker gangs, kept a code of silence in dealing with authorities. They spread the word around the EBC that they would settle scores with the Excelsiors in due time. The residents of the commune, in turn, had nothing of value to pass along to the police.

"I have no doubt it was payback for the Zodiacs burning the Kilrushes' property," Clemens stared at the deserted area around the barn. There were dozens of holes from where stakes had been pulled out of the ground, and debris was scattered about. Yet there wasn't anything that would warrant a police investigation, especially with all the numerous issues they faced in restoring a semblance of order in TrC. "If we don't have any witnesses or evidence, we don't have anything to go on. And it sure isn't a crime to leave town."

"I'd like to know where they lit off to," Roquefort stared out at the hills further west. "I wouldn't be surprised if they holed up in some of those caves or hollows out there. It'd be hard for the Zodiacs to come at them out there without getting spotted a mile off. They would've had to prepare something like that in advance. Elsewise, how the heck would they be able to feed all those kids out there?"

"Maybe we can send a chopper out there to see if they spot anything. At least we'll know where to go looking if anything else breaks out."

"I knew things were going to start going bad when those outlaw bikers started rolling in from Arizona and Texas after the bombings," Roquefort scowled. "These kids out here are just punks. Those outlaws, though, they brought a lot of bad experience with them. They fill our kids' heads with big ideas, and pretty soon they're gonna be out there firing guns at each other. We need to stop it now before it gets out of hand."

"Well, you and your boys can try and put a little pressure on the Zodiacs to make sure they don't go on the warpath," Clemens decided. "I think I'm gonna do a little poking around and find out where Mark Excelsior and his boys're pitching their tents."

Devin Kilrush would have never dreamed that very night would be his last as a member of the Excelsior Motorcycle Club.

Mark had given his new confidants the order to make the cavern at Devil's Holler ready to move into. Brute, Animal, Skull and Cueball had modified four sidecars for hauling, and they were able to bring resources to the cavern to get the job started. They looted a number of stores along south TrC and brought out sacks of rice, potatoes, beans and flour. Plastic-lined storage bins were built so that pests and vermin could not ruin the food supplies. They hauled out remodeling supplies and framed out partitions, painting the cave walls black and red. Within a few weeks, everything was ready for the rest of the gang and the kids from the commune to come in and finish the job.

Everyone was excited about the move, and the kids who had remained with the commune were of like mind with the bikers. They were greatly impressed with the Gothic theme of the cavern and the mystical symbols painted in gold and silver on the walls. Devin was somewhat perplexed by the dais set up at the rear of the cavern, and the altar that had been built upon it. There was a large pentagram painted on the dais, but Devin was well aware of Mark's recent fascination with the occult. He also knew that it was strengthening the bonds between the club and the campers, most of who were into black metal and the supernatural.

It was around midnight when things went sideways between Devin and Mark. They had not spoken much since the attack on the EBC. Devin was of the understanding that the club was going to stage the attack in order to draw out the Zodiacs. He was unaware that the bikers, particularly the new guys, would hit the commune as hard as they did. They had agreed that the flares would be used to light the camp up to improve visibility. There had been no talk about tossing them on top of the campers' tents. There had also been assaults and sexual abuse that Mark did not address when they returned to camp. Everybody was jubilant about how the attack on Devin's home had been avenged, but Devin was not good on how it went down.

He was sitting on a rock alongside his sleeping bag near where his pup tent and duffel bags sat. He watched as the band was trying to reassemble the generator that had been brought up from the McBride farm. Most of the guys were sitting around drinking moonshine, smoking and gambling as usual. Only he could see a few of the guys setting up candles and placing items up on the altar. At length Mark spread the word to have everyone gather around the altar.

"Brothers, tonight we celebrate the opening of our new headquarters here at Devil's Holler," Mark announced. "This is going to be the new center of power here in TrC. From here we are going to become the true rulers of Sierra County. We know that the police, the sheriff's department and the city council has lost their muscle. The Federal and State Government have left them hanging. What runs the streets now is biker power, and we already showed the Zodiacs what we got. Men, we are now the law in Sierra County, and all we need to do is get stronger every day!'

The cavern echoed with the whoops and whistles of the biker crew as they watched Brute and Animal bring forth a pig with its legs tied together. They lifted the animal and dropped it on the altar as it kicked and squealed.

"Boys, we are going to have ourselves a roast pork dinner tonight!" Mark announced, holding a jeweled dagger overhead. "You are gonna be dining better than most of the people you know in TrC! Now, we are gonna join hands in a special ceremony to Mormo, the King of the Ghouls! I will sacrifice this pig in his honor, and we shall dedicate this feast to him so that he can bless all our future endeavors. He will watch our backs as we take over Sierra County in his name!"

Mark watched as all the members but Devin gathered around the altar. He beckoned to Devin, who refused to come forth. Mark proceeded nonetheless in reading an arcane spell from a worn antique book as the boys joined hands. Brute then handed the dagger back to Mark, who gave him the book before driving the dagger into the ribcage of the pig. The animal squealed and bellowed but died shortly after its heart was pierced.

Once the ritual ended, the bikers took the pig from the altar, then butchered it quickly before impaling it on a spit and hoisting it over a fire. Mark and his inner circle walked over to where Devin had retired to his sleeping bag.

"So what's the story, Dev?" Mark stood with hands on hips as he stood before Devin. "We go out and settle your score, then you walk away from us?"

"It didn't take long for everything to change once we got in here," Devin sat on one of his duffel bags, looking up at him. "I kinda wonder how that all went down. Was that hit on the Zodiacs just a reason to break camp and come up here?"

"You know I told you I was gonna even things with the Zodiacs. I also told you we were gonna make this move. I didn't see any reason why we couldn't do it all in one shot."

"Now you're talking about 'we' and 'us'. How is it you let these saddletramps squeeze between us?"

"Why don't we step outside and see who's the saddletramp?" Brute growled.

"You just walked away from our ceremony," Mark glowered. "You're the vice-president of this club. That's just unacceptable."

"Nobody ever said anything about making sacrifices to the Devil. You and I always agreed on everything. We never said we were coming to stay out here, at least not anytime soon. Looks to me like you've been doing all your planning with these goons lately."

"You know better than to be hacking on ranking officers of this club," Mark pointed accusingly. "I wouldn't tolerate it any more than if they were coming up against you."

"You just created these offices since they joined the club. All of a sudden we have a counselor and a warlord. This is looking a lot more like a gang than a biker club. Don't you see that's what this is all about? Both of us know it has nothing to do with the Devil. What you don't realize is that it's about selling your soul."

"I think you spent too much time over at that church with those holy rollers. You let them take your girl away from you, and now you're losing your guts over them. I think you're gonna have to make a choice here."

"I already have," Devin rose to his feet. "I'm not choosing the church over the club. You're choosing to turn this club into a gang. I'm not gonna stay here and watch it happen."

"You're just gonna walk out on me, after all we've accomplished?" Mark was taken aback.

"We built this *club* into what it is. I don't know what you're planning to do with this *gang*, and I don't care."

"People don't just walk away from biker clubs, Mark," Cueball sneered as Devin began gathering his belongings. "You let him turn his back on us like that, you send a message to everyone else. If you let people show us their backside just like that, you let them disrespect our colors. Anyone who walks out needs to run the gauntlet, brother."

"That's right, punk," Brute snarled at Devin. "We stuck our necks out for you at the EBC. You owe us, and you don't just walk out without paying the tab."

"So which one of your goons do I take on to walk out of here?" Devin stared at Mark.

"Take your pick," Brute growled as he and his three partners walked over to the cavern entrance and spread out alongside one another.

"So this is how it ends," Devin took off his club jacket and handed it to Mark.

"It's not what I want," Mark shook his head.

Devin swaggered over to the four bikers, then cracked his neck and rolled his shoulders. He did a couple of squats to warm his legs up before launching himself into the line like the linebacker of old. He slammed into Brute, ramming him flat on his back. At once the others surrounded him, kicking and stomping him with their heavy boots. After knocking him into semi-consciousness, Animal stood him up as they beat him with their fists. Mark finally interceded when the blood was dripping from Devin's face.

"Okay, that's it," Mark announced as the other club members had crowded around. "You're outta here. Toss him and the rest of his stuff outside next to his bike. Don't ever come back, Devin. Ever."

The bikers dragged him out and dumped him alongside his Harley. They brought his gear out and dropped it on top of him before he finally blacked out.

Chapter Seven

"So is this heaven?"

"Many of the residents of Truth or Consequences would think so. Yet it is afflicted by human frailty just as every other place on Earth. It was decided that you should see this, not just for your own edification, but to better understand the complexities of man."

"May I take your order, gentlemen?"

John and Azrael looked up at the beautiful Greek waitress awaiting their command. They were sitting on the patio at the Oasis, a luxurious restaurant overlooking Grikos Bay. The beach area was particularly idyllic, lined by tamarisk trees affording a breathtaking view of its crystal-clear waters. Beyond the bay was Kalikatsou, its rolling peak considered as a natural monument. John remembered the view as being the very walls that would imprison him for the rest of his life. It was only now that he could appreciate its majestic beauty.

"What would you suggest?"

"The lamb is excellent today. Would you like some wine with that?"

"Certainly, my dear."

"You can see how those in Truth or Consequences would be sympathetic to your own history," Azrael said as he sipped his ice water. He wore a beautiful white suit that seemed translucent, made of material to be found nowhere on earth. His curly blond hair and well-trimmed beard appeared to be sprinkled with gold, and people could not help but stare at him as they passed. Even John was astounded by how beautiful his face appeared. "They too once saw their land as a place of wonderment. Now they see it as a prison, a place of desolation, just as you once saw this very place."

"They have more hope than I do," John was wistful. "I could remain here—there—a hundred years and never see it become what it is now."

"This is what you have to convey to them," Azrael said gently.

"Will we—look like you in the hereafter?"

"Much better looking. You are made in the image and likeness of God. We are mere angels."

"The Scripture says that a thousand years is as a day to Almighty God," John slowly stirred sweetener into his coffee. "Here—there—a day is like a thousand years. I would prefer not to go back there."

"Do you remember those things you had written? In the Scripture?"

"No. No, I do not. Somehow I knew the words were mine, but, no, I do not remember.

"That is because they had yet to be written. You must return so that the Christ's plan can be perfected in you."

"Will I—remember this? I'm sure it would make it all the more easier."

"You are part of all this," Azrael waved his hand. "You are part of the Body of Christ, and He is Master of the Universe. Therefore, all of it is part of you. Boundaries of space and time are part of your corporeal limitations. Once your mind, body and spirit are one, just as He is One, nothing will be hidden from you. Yet even now your spirit yearns for its freedom under Christ. When you look at this when you are restored to where you were, somewhere inside you will know, and it will help you believe."

"Why us?" John ran his fingers through his hair. "Why me?"

"Who can understand the things of God? What use would it be for the pot to ask the potter, 'Why hast thou made me thus'? Why was I not made—like you?"

"Are we—are we all going back once this is over?"

"Yes. Peter and Paul will return to Rome, and Simon to Lebanon. Neither will they remember, but deep in their subconscious, they will know. Just like you."

"These things are too hard," John buried his face in his hands. At once he had a vertiginous sensation, and held onto his face as if it would keep him from disappearing into the vortex of a black hole in space—

"Say, brother, are you okay? It seems to have been a restless night for you."

John looked around in confusion and saw Paul standing over his mattress in concern. He was back at the church, and he could see Peter and Simon collecting their gear for the day ahead.

"What are you doing?" John rubbed his face. "Where are you going?"

"We are going to one of the churches in Teer Cee to meet with the lost sheep," Paul explained. "Katia and her friends organized it for us. They are in great pain and in need of direction. This is our opportunity to help them make all things new through Christ."

"I—I was given a vision," John revealed as he rose to his feet.

"As were we all," Paul smiled. "I was transported back to Rome, as was Peter. It was quite impressive to see what they've done to the place. Simon got to visit Beirut. He was assured that he was taken to the better part of town."

"It was Azrael who met with me, the Angel of Death," John managed.

"Yes, he does get around, doesn't he? Did he take you to dinner?"

"It was lunch, actually. The food never arrived at our table."

"You're not alone. I had barely taken a couple of bites of my *cannoli*."

A minivan bearing the words *Grace Christian Church* arrived at the camp a short time later. The four men piled inside along with Katia, Mary and Martha. They drove into the city, and the men got their first look at the devastation. The mini-nuke was delivered in the form of a suitcase bomb which leveled buildings as far as seven hundred yards from the center of town. The church was just outside the blast radius, and only the facades of the buildings across the street remained as Hollywood mockups.

The four men were impressed by the church, which was much larger than the one they inhabited. It was a three-story building with a marble veneer, and enormous plate glass windows that displayed the entire lobby and stairwell to the upper floors. They were all impressed by the giant cross outside, that reached from the second level to the roof. The driver, who claimed to be an elder, led them inside to where the congregation awaited.

There were nearly a hundred people in attendance, and it was revealed that they were members of different churches in town whose membership had relocated to Albuquerque. It appeared that a higher proportion of the laity remained behind to pick up the pieces of their lives. There was great resentment towards those who they considered to have fled. They regarded the church leaders as hypocrites and came out to meet the four men with great reluctance.

The leader of the meeting introduced himself as Chaplain Steve Clinton. He was the minister at Sierra Vista Hospital, and had battled demonic spirits that had plagued the facility for decades. After the bombings, he had nearly given up hope until the four men arrived. He sent word to see if the rumors were true and now that they were here he turned the meeting over to them.

"Fellow Christians," Paul stood at the pulpit on the stage of the 1,000-seat facility. "We were sent here by Christ to lift your spirits and prepare you for the process of healing your land. There are great battles ahead of you, and we will wage war on your behalf. Nevertheless, it will be yours to defend the ground which we capture for your sake to the glory of Christ."

"So have you come here to take out terrorists?" the crowd asked.

"Your armies have set forth to subdue the enemies of this world. We are here to destroy the strongholds of the demons that have crushed your spirits and quenched your faith."

"I don't think it was demons that up and ran off, leaving us high and dry," an older man called out.

"Your church leaders were not strong enough to hold this ground. That is why we were sent."

"So we come back here and get to praying, and what's it gonna do?" another man demanded. "We were here every week praying with our families, and it didn't do us a lick of good. This town's been leveled, there's barely enough food to go around and we can't earn a living. If God couldn't help us in our time of need, what's He gonna do now?"

"Are you any different than those whose homes were flooded during storms, or collapsed by earthquakes? If all other Christians abandoned their faith in times of trouble, I am sure there would have been no one to even build this church."

"People talk about 9/11, they only lost two thousand people. We lost three thousand right here, not to count all the people who got crippled by that blast. Even if the town got back to normal, half of us still wouldn't be able to work again!"

"The greatest test of character comes when the spirit is willing but the flesh is weak. Here perhaps the opposite is true. Let us see if that is so. Those of you who have been injured, come forth and see whether he who is in the world can contend with He Who created it."

The four watched as half the audience began rising from their pews. Some used canes to move around, and others were on crutches. Many had their hearing impaired by the explosion, while others had suffered eye damage. Still others were hit by flying debris and suffered internal injuries that the overwhelmed hospitals had yet to deal with.

"Well, you asked for it," Peter muttered.

"You have seen men raised from the dead," Paul replied. "I haven't seen anyone carried in here thus far."

"I saw a Man rise from the dead and ascend into Heaven," Peter said proudly.

"Then this shall be child's play for Him," Paul grunted as he proceeded to climb down from the stage to meet the procession. His companions followed him down to the church floor.

Katia, seated in the front row, watched in astonishment as the disabled came forth and had hands laid upon them by the men. At once those who were lame tossed their crutches aside, and others tossed their slings away as they flexed their arms in amazement. Neck and back braces were discarded as men rushed back to their loved ones to share their joy with friends and family.

"I've backslid, brother," Chaplain Clinton approached Peter with tears in his eyes. "Help my unbelief."

"You've turned to drink, and it avails you naught." Peter said gruffly. "Be not drunk with alcohol, but with the Holy Ghost Who costs you nothing but faith. From here on, every drop you drink will taste twice as bitter, and you will remember this day should you force yourself to drink enough to make a fool of yourself."

"Thank you, brother, thank you," Steve hugged Peter tightly.

"Sir, there is a brother in the back who was brought here against his will," a man came to Paul. "His wife and children were killed in the blast, and his body was crushed though he survived. We brought him in a wheelchair, but now the wheels have locked up and we cannot budge him."

"Pick up the chair and bring him here," Paul looked to the rear where four men stood around a wheelchair at the back of the church.

"It seems impossible, but it will not budge. Those four strong men cannot lift it."

"Nonsense," Paul came out and stood in the main aisle. "Tell them to step aside."

Paul stretched his hand out towards the man, and at once the wheelchair was drawn slowly towards the stage though the wheels did not move at all. The disabled man's eyes bulged as if he would have resisted, yet the chair continued along the aisle until it stopped in front of Paul and the others.

"He seems to have a problem," Peter observed.

"It is clear he cannot speak," Paul replied.

"Feel his head."

"Does he have a fever as well?"

"If you feel his head you can probably read his mind better. I believe he does not want your help."

"I feel his anger," John spoke up. "He is upset with the Lord because he feels he should have died with his loved ones."

"Are you suggesting we leave him as is?" Paul insisted.

"He is confused, brothers," Simon interjected. "If you remember those who were afflicted by demons, they even rejected help from Jesus Himself. Let him be cured so that he can regain his faith and show others what Christ has done."

"Very well then," Paul folded his arms, "have at it."

"Why, thank you," Simon smiled, then turned to the man. "In the name of the Lord Jesus Christ, take that wheelchair and bring it to one who has use of it."

A great cry rose from the congregation as the man stiffly lifted his arms and legs from the braces on the chair, unbuckling the straps that held him in place.

"Why was I not killed along with the rest of my family?" the man rose and came before Peter. "My life has no meaning without them."

"The Lord has work for you to do," Peter replied. "Close your eyes and you will see where they await you."

Peter took hold of the man's head on either side, and the others watched as his expression slowly changed from one of grief to unadulterated joy. At once he dropped on his face and hugged Peter's ankles, weeping over his boots.

"You'd best not move until he lets go," John patted him on the shoulder. "It could prove embarrassing." Peter gave him a playful scowl as he watched the others walk down the aisle.

"Now you have seen the power of the Lord," Paul exhorted them. "Now you can go back to your family and friends and tell them the Lord never left you. He has been here providing you with strength and protection all along. Here He has shown you that even the Devil's most vicious attacks are but in vain. Behold how He makes all things new. So shall Teer Cee arise from the ashes and become stronger than ever before."

"Will you—will you raise the very buildings?" an old man asked.

"No, but you will bring your families together," John told him. "Your city is not the buildings, but the homes that make them worthy. We will send your children back to you, and you will be reconciled to them so that you can re-build."

"Some of the kids are still in the biker camps," another man spoke up.

61

"This is the end of our labor, the hard part that lies ahead," Peter came forth as he helped the healed man to his feet. "The Devil has a strong grip on those children that must be broken. Tonight we will return to the church with Katia and the girls, and we will inform those within that you are expecting them home. Tomorrow we will prepare to set the others free."

"They left because we weren't able to make ends meet," the crowd was forlorn. "They could not stick around and watch us starve."

"I will meet you at the lake at daybreak along with some of the children," Peter replied. "They will show you what we have taught them, and you will renew your relationship with them. You will bring back more than enough fish to feed your families."

"But the Government reported all the fish in the lake were dead," the healed man came up behind them.

"Just as they said you could not walk," Paul smiled.

And so they remained praising God for the rest of the afternoon before returning to their homes.

The Elephant Butte Commune was just starting to pick up the pieces after the Excelsior attack. The Zodiacs were coming out and mingling with the residents, flirting with the girls and keeping a high profile. Most of the hippie old-timers saw it as too little too late, but were glad they were out providing security nonetheless. They cajoled some of the bikers in helping with minor chores when necessary. The hippies ended up doing most of the heavy lifting, bringing canvas in from town to get as many tents up in short order.

Hakeem Mogambo watched the hippies cutting out a length of canvas from a bolt purloined from a sail manufacturing company. This tit-for-tat war with the Excelsiors was not working out for the Zodiacs. They had been stealing from each other's camps ever since the bombing, and finally a gang war was called to settle it. The Excelsiors came out on top in a battle that attracted the TCPD's attention. The attack on Devin Kilrush's home was supposed to be payback. Not only did it bring the TCPD down on them, but it caused this hit on the EBC that was a major loss of face. There was now a question of if they could defend the EBC adequately. If the hippies decided to switch allegiance to the Excelsiors, all could be lost out here.

Mogambo watched as a lone biker approached from the west, driving slowly but deliberately directly towards where he sat on his bike. This was entirely unexpected and he was unsure if this fellow intended to launch a sneak attack.

Something like this would precipitate a retaliatory attack against the Excelsiors in broad daylight that would result in police intervention. Possibly those big lazy dogs in the National Guard might even come out. Mogambo had no choice but to let this stranger play his hand.

"Whuzzup, Hakeem?" the biker slowed to a halt.

"Man, you gots to be crazy coming out here like this. What happened to your face?"

"The boys and I had a bit of a disagreement," Devin Kilrush got off his bike. He wore a cutoff denim jacket which replaced his Excelsior colors. "Now take me to your leader."

Jhonny Rodz stood by a shed in a clearing surrounded by some of his confidants. He chose to remain at a distance from the residents to emphasize his authority over the commune and the bike club. His expression alarmed his entourage, and they whirled to stare at Devin as he was escorted by Hakeem into their midst.

"What happened to your face, dude?" Rodz sniggered. "You do something to get that little Christian girl of yours to drop her cross?"

"Leave her out of this," Devin stopped a couple of feet before him, hooking his thumbs in his belt.

"Dog, you just walked into the lions' den. I say what I like. I'll make you think you look like Brad Pitt right now when we get through with you."

"I think you wanna hear what I have to say first."

"I *knows* what you gots to say. Marky Boy decided you more trouble than you worth. He kicked you out on your ear and you gonna come begging here."

"You didn't get to be President of this club by being stupid," Devin caused the hackles to rise on their necks. "Sure I wanted payback on you guys for burning my parents' shed down. My Dad's tools got burned up in that fire. That was his livelihood. Those were tools he collected over thirty years. He's not going to be able to get the money to replace those tools. Plus, there were dogs in that shed. Dogs that I raised from puppies. Dogs that got burned alive in that fire. I didn't come here to beg, Jhonny. If I wanted more than Mark was willing to give me, I would've been up in those hills with a hunting rifle taking out anything I saw wearing Zodiac colors. No, I quit the club because *they* wanted too much. Mark has dreams of taking control over all TrC. You got that right, Jhonny Rodz. I got a little Christian girl out there, and my parents are still out there. Eventually they're gonna be standing on ground that Mark wants to control. I tried to stand in his way and this is how he dealt with it. Now I'm coming here to see if you're gonna try and stop him."

"Payback's a witch, ain't it," Jhonny shook his head. "Now whatchoo think you bringing to my table that's gonna help me take down the Excelsiors?"

"You gotta know better than to ask a question like that," Devin was cocksure. "I helped Mark Excelsior build that club. I was the one who gave the club its name. I built that man's ego up, I convinced him that he could build a club that could stand up against the biker gangs that come riding through here. I'm the man that stood behind the throne, I'm the one who whispered into the king's ear. I created all their strategies, I know how they attack and how they defend. I played football beside this man. I know everything he's got inside, I know what he can do and what he cannot do. *This* is what I bring to your table, Jhonny Rodz."

"Okay, dude," Jhonny relented. "You got my attention."

"You let me come in as a club officer, no initiation. I'll earn my place on the field. Mark's withdrawn to Devil's Holler. He's got the club and the commune side by side in the cavern out there. I know the layout, I know how we can get in there and take them out."

"Whatchoo mean, take them out? How I know you ain't come here to lure me into a trap?"

"Get real, dude. I'm gonna be out there right alongside you. If you get caught, I'll already be at your mercy. If we get caught, how are they gonna take you out without taking me? Look, if we sit here and do nothing, he'll be going to take out that church next. After he takes that, he'll be coming to take the EBC. If he takes the EBC, he's gonna be looking at South TrC next. The people who live in these neighborhoods will have no choice but to let him raise his flag up there. When the cops recognize his authority, it's all over. You'll never be able to move against him after that."

"What's your plan?" Hector Alindato spoke up.

"Got a jacket for me?" Devin looked at each of them.

"Get the man a jacket," Jhonny smirked. "I think we gonna start planning a housewarming party for Devin's old friends."

Chapter Eight

After a lengthy discussion, the four men were driven back to the church early that evening. The congregation had spread the word that all Christians of TrC were to meet at Ground Zero outside of the blast perimeter. Though remaining under watch by the National Guard, they did nothing to discourage the people as they gathered along the downtown area for what was scheduled to be a prayer meeting.

Peter had asked that they rally all Christians to assemble in the downtown area. The believers explained the situation in detail and drove the four to Ground Zero. They were told to call their fellow churchgoers to the vicinity for a prayer rally. They would then join in prayer and ask God to heal their land. Once word had gotten out about the miraculous healing that had transpired less than an hour ago, the community was galvanized so that hundreds of people began making their way downtown.

Before long, the word had spread as to what the apostles had planned. They wanted to have enough people to be able to join hands in a circle that would completely surround Ground Zero. This resulted in many more residents coming out to participate in the event. The National Guardsmen watched in bemusement as the crowds thickened along the downtown area, and soon a couple of broadcast vehicles from local radio stations came out to provide live coverage. Eventually it was estimated nearly half the population had turned out.

"It was said that the leaders of the Christian church had forsaken the people of Truth or Consequences," Paul spoke into a microphone that had been provided by a mobile recording station dispatched to the site by a nearby recording studio. They had erected columns of speakers and horns through which the apostles could address the multitude. "Anyone familiar with Scripture knows that when Christian leaders falter, God merely raises others to take their place. It was said that God had turned His back on His people and forsaken them in their time of tribulation. Rest assured He has strengthened them, and as we can see, the spirit of Christianity in Truth or Consequences is stronger than ever. It was said that the church here in TrC has drifted apart and could never be rebuilt. Know for sure, brothers and sisters, that upon this Rock the Church was built, and the gates of Hell shall never prevail against it!"

Paul turned the mic over to Peter, and the roar of the crowd was such as if there was a professional sports competition taking place in the city streets.

"There had been a lot of talk about how families had been ripped apart by the catastrophe here in Truth of Consequences," Peter looked out at what had turned out to be a crowd of over three thousand people, as many as had come out for New Year's Eve several months ago. "It seems to me that if all those families had been ripped apart, then the Spirit of God has not wasted much time in putting them back together. There had been a lot of talk about how the city of Truth of Consequences could no longer provide for its families, and that homes were being torn apart because this city could not survive. Let me tell you something: cities do not provide for families. Governments do not provide for families. God provides for families, and all you have to do is ask and you will receive. Now, as for all that talk about children having to leave home because their parents were unable to take care of them, it seems to me that there are quite a few children out here with their parents today!"

When the teens at the church camp heard what the apostles were doing in TrC, many of them came into town to see what was happening. Soon the word spread like wildfire, and dozens of kids from EBC arrived to share in the festivities. As a result, children were finding their families in the crowd and reunions broke out everywhere.

"As it is written, to everything there is a season," Peter handed the mic to Simon, who climbed up onto a flatbed truck that rolled up alongside the sound mobile unit. Simon walked to the edge of the flatbed as he addressed the jubilant crowd. "There is a time of war, and a time of peace. There is a time to break down, and a time to build up. There is a time to mourn, and a time to dance. There is a time to gain, and a time to lose. There is a time to plant, and a time to reap. Well, let me tell you, the time of war is over. The time of breakdown, the time of mourning, the time of loss is over. The time of peace has come. The time to rebuild is here, and it's now time to rejoice in what the Lord has restored here in TrC! Let's hear it from the Son of Thunder, the Revelator himself!"

"It is written," John took the mic to a deafening ovation, "that the apostle John was the disciple that Jesus loved. Well, let me tell you something. The Lord Jesus Christ loves each and every one of you who have gathered here in His name today! We have come here to witness how He has come into your lives to reclaim your city, reclaim your families and reclaim your land. Now, if there's any doubt as to how to go about reclaiming your land, I want you all to follow Paul and Peter in walking around this downtown area giving praise to Almighty God!"

The National Guardsmen watched moodily as the huge crowd began to join the line, proceeding in both directions until Peter met Paul not far from where they had started. The lieutenants in command of the units assigned to the downtown area called their command centers and reported that Ground Zero was entirely encircled by the residents. The soldiers grew wary as the throng began joining hands, then bowed their heads and became engrossed in prayer. They looked around, remaining alert lest terrorists used the spectacle as a diversion.

Next their radios began squawking as multiple broadcasts began coming in simultaneously. The Colonel in command gave immediate orders that the units delay their transmissions so that instructions could be heard clearly on the airwaves. It was determined that there were numerous breakdowns of Geiger counters and radiation monitors along the perimeter. Upon further investigation, it was reported that the instruments appeared to be in working order though indicating the radiation count in downtown TrC had dropped to zero.

At length a helicopter came in from Albuquerque, and its monitoring equipment was checked to be in perfect order. The crew confirmed that the radiation readings in TrC were now at acceptable levels. The commanding officer, Colonel Kellogg, had accompanied the chopper crew to investigate the situation. He was briefed on the incidents surrounding the prayer meeting and ordered that the apostles be brought before him.

"Which one of you is in charge here?" the Colonel asked as a squad of riflemen escorted him to the flatbed where Chaplain Clinton was now leading the crowd in prayer.

"He is," Peter and Paul pointed at one another.

"Okay, we'll do it your way. Which one is Peter?"

"I am."

"Do you know how this area was decontaminated so rapidly?"

"Yes."

The colonel exchanged glances with a major, and they stared at Peter who offered no further explanation.

"Well, sir, as you know, other cities here in New Mexico have also endured nuclear attacks that have caused similar levels of contamination as these people have suffered here. Is there something that you and your friends can do to minimize radiation levels elsewhere?"

"What part of this do you not understand?" Peter wondered. "The people prayed to the Lord, and it was God Who healed their land. We merely redirected the people's attention to God. If all your cities unite in prayer, all your cities can be healed."

"I'll be sure and pass that along. Sir, we appreciate what you have done here today."

"Praise God," Peter corrected him.

Almost an hour later and five miles away, Dick Wynter had come home after a grueling day at the Government Recycling Center. He had brought in a truckload of cardboard, plastic and paper sacks, spending half the day in a long queue of vehicles to have his items weighed for payment. He had risen well before dawn to begin scavenging and finally filled his truck by noon. He endured the desert sun in his truck for the rest of the time, eating buttered bread and sipping flavored water as he waited his turn. They finally processed his items by dusk, and he brought ten dollars home when he pulled into the driveway. It would pay for about a quarter tank of gas tomorrow.

He walked up the pathway and could hear voices inside. He rolled his eyes in exasperation, certain that one of Jane's friends had come by. He only hoped she had prepared dinner, managed to scrape up enough for stew somehow. All he wanted to do was take a shower and go to bed. This routine was killing him, and the only word from the Government was that they might be hiring for the Workforce next month. They would need diggers to remove debris from downtown if radiation counts had dropped to acceptable levels. He only hoped his back would hold out that long. He hoped he would get hired among all the applicants.

"Daddy!"

The light in Dick's eyes returned briefly as Katia ran to meet him at the door, like she did back in the old days before the bombing. Like she did back before the madness had literally blown his maintenance company away in the blast downtown, back before she decided to move out when he could no longer provide for three people. He had fantasized about picking up a gun and robbing a bank to get the money he needed to support his wife and daughter. Only there was not even a place left worth robbing. Besides, a bank guard would probably take him out with one shove. He had lost fifteen pounds making sure his wife had enough to eat.

"Hello, honey," he hugged his daughter, delighted that she still seemed healthy. At least the kids at the commune were getting enough to eat. "Are you doing okay?"

"I'm just fine, Daddy," she kissed his face, trying to keep from crying over his haggard appearance. "I brought a friend I want you to meet."

"Well, let me jump in the shower right quick," he insisted. "I don't—smell too good right now."

"That won't be necessary," the sturdily-built, dark-haired man rose from the couch in the spacious living room. "I won't be staying long. You'll want to be spending your time with your wife and child. I believe a celebration is in order."

"Celebration?" he managed a chuckle, looking back and forth from the visitor to Katia to Jane.

"Daddy, this is Paul," she said as he stepped forth and shook Dick's hand. "He's one of the men I told you about who moved into the church on the south side."

"Pleased to meet you. I'd like to thank you personally for getting Katia to move away from that biker gang. I feel a lot more comfortable knowing she's camping out by you folks."

"She has come home to stay," Paul revealed. "She'll go back to the camp in the morning to collect her belongings. She will be able to give you more information about the camp. I believe it will be far easier to make a living there."

"Well, wait a second," Dick was perplexed. "How did all this come about? She seems to be doing pretty good out there, and frankly—I've having a little trouble making ends meet here. I don't want to burden you with my troubles—"

"The Lord will see to it that your troubles are ended."

"I—uh," Dick tried to remain calm. "You know, pal, I don't mean any disrespect…"

"Mrs. Wynter," Paul turned to her, "you have a red container in your refrigerator. You also have a metal breadbox in your kitchen. Please bring them here."

"What is this?" Dick managed a chuckle. "Are you a magician?"

Katia followed her mother into the kitchen and brought the breadbox out to Paul. He directed them to place the items on the coffee table.

"I would suggest that you praise God every day of your life for His blessings," Paul told them. "It will remain a symbol of the Lord's covenant with this family. You must never open the container to check its contents, and neither shall you open the breadbox to look inside. Otherwise the blessing of that container will end on that very day. Likewise will your storage box that holds your meat shall never break down as long as it belongs to you."

"Why, the—" Jane reached over to jiggle the milk container, and was taken aback to find it was full. She instinctively rushed to the kitchen to retrieve glasses as Katia lifted the hatch of the breadbox, which had grown warm to the touch. She pulled out a loaf of bread and took a bite, sighing with satisfaction at the taste. The only time she had ever eaten bread like this was at the church, the day Simon showed the girls how to bake bread on the barbecue grill.

"Neither shall you tell anyone of these things, or the blessing will end. This is a covenant between the Lord and this family."

Jane poured a glass of milk for each of them, and nearly dropped the container in trepidation. The container remained full.

"Daddy?" Katia brought a glass of milk and a loaf of bread over to her father, trying to keep her hands from shaking. Every time she took a small loaf from the breadbox, it was full when she reopened it.

"How are you—?" Dick began when all of a sudden he heard a click and a hum from the basement. He knew it was the meat freezer downstairs. Only the freezer had been disconnected after the motor blew up a month ago.

"Oh my gosh," Jane sat on the couch, burying her face in her hands. "Oh my gosh."

At once they heard a truck pull up out in front of the house, and Dick could see its emergency lights flickering through the window curtains. They could hear its door rumbling open, and at length a man came up the walkway and rang the doorbell. Jane got up and rushed to answer.

"Delivery, ma'am," a tall, robust man in a white uniform announced.

"Take it downstairs, please," Paul directed him. The man brought in two huge white sacks over five feet in length, carrying them as if they were filled with feathers. He walked past them to the basement steps without as much as looking around the room.

"What—where?" Dick managed as Jane scurried behind the man, following him downstairs.

"There is enough meat to last for some time," Paul explained. "By the time it runs out, you will have collected on your insurance policy and started a new venture. Everything works out to the glory of God."

"Who are you?" Dick stared in disbelief. "Where did you come from?"

"Praise God from Whom all blessings flow," Paul turned to leave, thanking the man in white who walked back out the door and drove off. "Thank Him daily for the blessings He has bestowed upon your family on this day."

"Please," Jane rushed over to him. "At least let me make you something to eat." Paul reached up and held her face gently in his hands, praying in a language never before spoken on Earth. At once she dropped back on the couch, slumping backwards and dazedly praising God.

"God bless you, sir," Dick whispered. "God bless you." Paul smiled and gestured towards him, and Dick stumbled to his armchair where he collapsed in prayer.

"Paul! Wait!"

"By the way," Paul turned to her as he started down the walkway. "Tell your father his back is fine."

"Paul, I'm scared. You're not leaving us, are you?" tears streamed down her cheeks.

"Come now, child, remember all you have learned," Paul stroked her face. "It is the Lord Jesus Christ Who remains with you for the rest of your days. Our work is done here. There remains but one task to be completed, then all four of us must return to the assignments from which we were called away."

"You can't leave," Katia buried her face against his chest as she wept. "You can't!"

"Your friend Devin is in great need of help," he stroked her hair gently. "Surely you will want us to intercede on his behalf. Beyond that, the Evil One has retired from Teer Cee and has taken refuge in the mountains. We must go there and evict him at once. Once he is thrown out to whence he came, our work is done."

"Paul, you can't go back, you can't. I remember what they taught us in school. If you go back to Rome you'll be killed, and so will Peter. And Simon dies in Beirut."

"Kat.a!" Paul chided her, holding her at arms' length. "How can you say such things? Do you not remember the Scriptures we studied together? Peter spoke thusly to the Lord Jesus Himself, and Christ looked over his shoulder to order the Devil to step away. We sleep not as men sleep, but are transformed in the blink of an eye. Remind all your friends of this when they mourn and weep for those they have lost in Teer Cee."

"Please don't leave without saying goodbye," she sobbed.

"For you I will make an exception," he kissed her forehead. She stood crying on the pathway as he continued across the lawn to the sidewalk. A gentle breeze swept past her, causing her to sneeze. When she opened her eyes, he had disappeared.

Devin checked his saddlebag and made sure his weapons were in place before he climbed onto his bike. They had made him the club treasurer, a dubious position that made him a club officer nonetheless. He looked around and saw fifty other bikers preparing to ride. Mark knew a shortcut to the west of Devil's Holler, through a dried gully concealed behind a stand of saguaro. Once they traversed a rocky incline cutting past the scrub and grassland, they could come around and catch them unawares through the adjoining conifer forest that would obscure their view.

'All right, guys," Jhonny emerged from the barn that served as their headquarters about a mile northwest of the EBC. "Let's get ready to rock and roll!"

He was met by a great roar and war whoops from the gang as they began revving their engines. Only they looked up along the rise at the entranceway along the fenceline surrounding the property and saw the four men standing in a line across the threshold.

"What the heck is that!" Hector Alindato yelled angrily.

Jhonny straddled his bike and cruised over to where Peter and Paul stood with their fists on hips.

"Now what do you fools think you're doing?" Jhonny demanded.

"We know where you are going and what you are planning!" Paul called out to them above the roar of the engines. "What you are about to do is illegal! We have brought the peace of the Lord to Teer Cee and we will not allow you to disturb it!"

"There's nothing you can do about it! After we run you over, we're going up to Devil's Holler and take out the Excelsiors!" Jhonny yelled back.

"It must be over ten miles to the Holler!" Paul replied. "If you walk all the way out there you will be too tired to fight."

Devin rode over to where Jhonny idled before the apostles. At once he had a bad feeling about this. He had no doubt these were men of God. He witnessed them repair Clyde's teeth, not only fixing his rotten tooth but straightening every other one in his mouth. He heard them speak, he felt their power. He would be risking his life to stand against Jhonny now, making a move against the war party. Yet he would not stand by and let them run the men over.

"Jhonny, we can't do this," Devin called to him.

"Don't even think about it, dog," Jhonny vented his rage on Devin. "You better talk to those dudes and get them outta our way or we gonna run them over!"

"Peter—Paul—," Devin called over. "He's right, you need to stand aside."

"You there!" Peter demanded. "Do you have no fear of God?"

"I don't see God up there. Just you," Jhonny was arrogant.

"Well, He sees you, and He does not like what He sees!"

"I think that's gonna be between me and Him," Jhonny smirked.

"Perhaps," Peter said as Paul nodded to him.

"Confess your sins to the Lord, and your sins will be forgiven," Paul told them as he waved his hand from side to side. He and the apostles turned away, the roars of the engines fading away as the men disappeared into the darkness. The bikers began yelling and cursing, dismounting their bikes and checking their engines furiously to determine what the problem was.

It took nearly a half hour before they discovered there was not one drop of gas in any of their motorcycles, or their gas cans or underground tanks. They were all bone dry as if never used before, and the bikers spent the rest of the night marveling over what had happened.

Chapter Nine

Devin Kilrush folded his Zodiac jacket and walked his bike off the club property. He expected someone to come up from behind and take him out. Apparently they didn't care less. They knew he was connected with those guys who evaporated every drop of gas on site. They weren't going to take a chance of the apostles doing something else. Maybe they could make bikes start disappearing. Maybe they could make people disappear.

He had gotten Jhonny to agree to hit the Excelsiors around 2330 that night. It was right around the time they would be setting up their witchcraft gear. They would have made this a big one. Maybe Mark might have even had the gang hit one of the closed-down amusement parks in Albuquerque and rip off a haunted house. He would be turning the cavern into his own spook show and hopefully lure some more metalheads and goth kids into his web. Maybe some of the kids at the church camp would get bored with all the Bible Schools stuff and come back in.

Devin tried to figure out how things went sideways between him and Mark. They were so close back in the day. Mark was the quarterback and Devin was the running back, high school football's version of Butch Cassidy and the Sundance Kid. They were that close off the field, bosom buddies, hoping they would get into the same University together. They agreed to buy Harleys and go riding the summer before they made their college picks. They found others of like mind and put the Excelsiors together. Shortly after, the terrorists attacked.

Most of the time it was just a case of sticking an idea into Mark's ear and making him think it was his own. They won lots of football games that way, and it was pretty well how they got the Excelsior Motorcycle Club up and rolling. Only some things took more time, and some things just wouldn't happen. Mark didn't like to think too much, and that's why it was so easy to stick ideas in his head. Things that created dissonance made his head hurt. Devin was forever careful to not to insert those kind of things.

Religion, philosophy, politics, big things like that didn't fit in Mark's ear-holes. All he could do was draw mental pictures and make them attractive enough to hold Mark's attention. Only Mark had an attention-deficit disorder and could easily get sidetracked. When the phony tough guys with the phony tough guy names came in and started feeding him all that mind candy, it wasn't long before he started seeing himself as King of the Monsters and the rebel leader of a biker army. Maybe the death metal bands had something to do with it, made him think he was the next Rob Zombie. It was all just a matter of time before he and Devin parted ways. Devin might have manipulated him at times, but he never blew smoke up his nose. Blood brothers didn't do things like that.

Maybe all that God stuff was how he and Mark broke up. If the Zodiacs never hit his parents' place, he would have never tried to get revenge by taking out the EBC. Taking out the EBC was bad karma. If they hadn't torched the EBC, there would have been no reason to abandon Stewy's and move out to Devil's Holler. If they hadn't moved, Mark probably wouldn't have bought into all that devil stuff to convince everyone they were going hardcore. One bad thing led to another, and if he would have followed Katia along the straight and narrow, Mark might have turned right instead of left.

He would never forgive Mark for making him run the gauntlet. Maybe the apostles were all about forgiveness, but Mark had gone too far. He and Mark had started the club. There should never have been a big deal about either of them walking out. The phony tough guys talked him into it so Devin would never come back. They were right about that. If Mark's pointy head caught fire in the middle of Main Street, Devin wouldn't have walked down the block to pour a cup of soda over it.

At length he grew tired from walking his bike over many miles on the way back to the church camp. He decided he would talk to the apostles and see about pitching a new tent out there. Maybe he would go back to his parents' home and try to work something out. He knew his Dad could use some help, and his Mom would be glad to have him back, especially after all their dogs having been killed. He needed to get together with Katia and start making some serious plans. He had lost too much in his life since the bombings, and the one thing he could not afford to lose was her.

He finally sat down beneath a sycamore tree, and a great tiredness over-whelmed him so that he was forced to close his eyes. He felt himself drifting to sleep and was unable to fight it off. He only prayed that the Excelsiors did not find him like this, or he would have no chance of fighting them off at all. He thought of Katia, imagining having her alongside him, cuddled under his arm. He remembered the fragrance of her hair, and thought of how much he loved her.

At once he felt a great wind sweeping across the valley, and he was in one of those sleep modes where one knew they were dreaming yet felt wide awake. He felt himself taken up over the valley, and it felt so real that he could see everything from over a hundred yards in the sky. He had never been up that high, so there was no way he could have known what it looked like. He soared over the valley and swirled towards Devil's Holler, and was dismayed to think that Mark had developed the power to transport others against their will.

He was deposited by the funnel cloud at the cavern entrance, where Katia and the apostles awaited. They were dressed in their robes and sandals as they were when they first met. He and Katia were dressed similarly, only their clothes were white as snow. Katia gave him a hug, yet the apostles' faces were grave as Paul motioned for them to lead the way inside.

The teens were astonished at the spectacle before them. The death metal bands' equipment had been set up around the dais in the clearing, and both the campers and the bikers were dressed in black with corpse paint on their faces. They were cheering and chanting as a pig had been tied to the altar, and Mark wore a priest's vestments for a Catholic funeral mass as he approached with a jeweled dagger. Behind him, the cavern filled with black smoke and mysterious lights that Devin had never seen before.

'Behold what your friends have prepared on this night,' Paul spoke as the apostles stood behind the teens.

'They're not my friends,' Devin insisted.

"They are your brethren. You must pray for them," Paul insisted.

"And who is this?" Mark's voice was as thunder throughout the cavern as he looked up and spotted the six figures at the cavern entrance. The scene grew quiet as the grave as they all turned and stared hatefully at the intruders. "What are you doing here?"

"The one you are inviting will not be staying," Paul called across the cavern. "He will be leaving, never to return."

"Throw those fools out of here," Mark commanded the bikers. "Let Devin and Katia stick around. I think we'll have some fun with them."

The bikers rushed up the incline towards the interlopers, and the apostles stepped forth in front of the young couple. As each biker approached to grab hold of the four men, they became paralyzed as Paul grabbed them by their heads and spoke in an unearthly language. The bikers fell at his feet as he pulled what appeared as globules of ectoplasm from their heads. He took each globule in his hand and flung them against the far wall. As they exploded, a demon screamed hideously before vanishing into thin air. The other apostles joined in until over a dozen bikers lay at their feet, the rest cowering in fear around them. The pig on the altar pulled free of its bonds and ran squealing into the darkness.

At that, the hair on both Devin and Katia's necks stood on end as they looked off to the left side of the cavern. They stared aghast as a crowd of thousands of demons were held at bay by a dozen white-robed men on horseback. The demons were sinewy as apes, their skins as black leather, with great wings as dragons sprouting from their backs. They had faces as gargoyles, their expressions filled with hatred and fury the like of which no man had ever seen. Their eyes were as burning lava as they stared directly at the young couple.

"They can't hold them!" Katia gasped as she beheld the horrid sight.

"Rest assured they will," Paul encouraged her. "They have been authorized by the Lord Jesus to do so. It is a tedious work, like keeping grain from spilling through a tear in a sack. Nevertheless, they will endure until we are done here."

"What business have you here, Paul of Tarsus?" a mighty voice thundered throughout the cavern. The residents and the bikers crawled away in terror as an amorphous mass billowed from behind the altar. Every mortal in the cavern hissed with fright as a black serpentine face with gleaming eyes and venomous fangs appeared translucent in the blackness. "This is our property according to Scripture! We have dominion over all the earth!"

"I ask you who is greater, he who rules the darkness or He Who created it?" Paul challenged him. "Tell me your name, dark monster!"

"I am the bright flame of evil, the hell fire that incinerates all! Mortals who seek my blessing will chant the name of Belial!" Paul knew the name from the fearsome and accursed *Lesser Key of Solomon*.

"I expel you in the name of the Lord Jesus Christ!" Paul charged him.

"And what will you accomplish in doing such a thing?" Belial taunted him. "These worshippers will merely find another place of worship and summon me anew. Furthermore, once this work is completed, the four of you will be returned to whence you came. There you will meet your appointed fate. Perhaps John is not concerned, being allowed to live out his days on a peaceful island. Perhaps you are not concerned, with your life to be snuffed in an instant. Yet Simon may not be as eager to be hewn in half by a saw. Nor will Simon Peter be as willing to he hung like a thief from a tree and suffer as did his Lord."

"A few minutes of pain, for sure, but afterwards to be rejoined with my Christ in heaven!" Simon retorted.

"So say you, Simon Peter?" the archdemon's eyes glowed in the shadows. "Even your great ego will not allow you to be crucified in the same manner as your Lord. You will be raised over the ground upside down, and there you will hang in agony until your heart explodes at last. Think of the spike that will secure your very ankles to the tree. It would be beyond the endurance of any man yet you will not be able to ignore the nails in your wrists. There will be no scourging for you, I am certain it will take far, far longer than three hours for you to die."

"Remember, Peter, that the very Church itself has been built by Christ upon His Rock," Paul spoke softly to him. "It is by your strength that the Church endures. The rest of us merely edify what the Christ has already established."

"Come, Peter, let us reason together," Belial called unto him. "Let us rest together before going our separate ways. I am in no great hurry to return to the void, as I am sure you do not make haste along your way to the cross."

"Paul, can't you ask Jesus to spare him?" Katia wept bitterly.

"With great power comes great responsibility," Paul replied. "Some of us are tested far more than others. This is what we must remember when confronting our own trials and tribulations. You and Devin must remember this night when counseling others."

"It's too much," Devin murmured. "It's not right."

"There were times when I would have chosen a cross instead of the scourgings I suffered," Paul allowed. "Yet it is our mission to accept what we are given."

"Nay, devil!" Peter's voice echoed throughout the cavern. "I would endure the cross a thousand times before one more minute in your hideous gaze! In the name of the Lord Jesus Christ I command you to leave this place, never to return!"

At once everyone in the cavern saw a clear vision of Peter hanging upside down on an inverted Roman cross, blood spilling down his legs as he gasped in unendurable torment.

"Bring it to me, Devil!" Peter roared. "Begone!"

There was a deafening explosion as the cavern blazed with a great light. Soon everyone regained their sight to discover that the space behind the altar was cleared. Before the far wall stood only a cordon of angels, and they disappeared as mist before their eyes. The bikers and the campers buried their faces in their hands, begging God for forgiveness.

"Omigosh," Katia wept as Devin held her in his arms. "Is it over?"

"No, my child," Paul put his hands on her shoulders. "It is only just begun. You must now bring these lost sheep to Christ, so that they may join you in bringing truth and faith into Teer Cee. There is much work ahead, but now you have seen and now you are ready."

"I don't know how to—", Katia began, but at once the apostles disappeared before her eyes.

Chapter Ten

The next day, newscasts on the miracles at Truth or Consequences resulted in many church workers from Albuquerque returning to town. Among these was the Board of Elders from the Sermon on the Mount Church on the southern outskirts of TrC. They found the vacated church having been restored by the apostles, and most of the campers having packed up and returned to their homes and families. All the Christians were astounded by the works of God, which inspired a revival as never before seen in Sierra County.

Devin and Katia met with the elders at the Grace Christian Church downtown, and they agreed to act as the leaders of the new Youth Outreach program. Many of the former members of the Excelsior Motorcycle Club and the commune joined the group, and they took to the streets in testifying to what they had witnessed at the cavern. More than a few people were skeptical, yet there was no denying the fervor of those who had once terrorized the south side of TrC.

The Kilrushes invited the Wynters to dinner that weekend, and Devin presented Katia with a ring in asking for their parents' approval. The two families were filled with delight as they agreed to the Christian bonding between their children. Katia was so overwhelmed with joy that she went outside to the backyard shortly afterward to collect her thoughts.

She looked up at the starry skies and thanked God for the blessings He had showered upon their families. She had never known such joy in her life, and resolved that she would devote herself to sharing the Good News with others.

"I told you I wouldn't leave without saying goodbye."

Katia whirled and at once threw herself into the arms of Paul, who stroked and kissed her hair.

"The Lord will always be with you and Devin, my child," he assured her. "He is pleased with what you have done and will forever bless what you do in His Name."

"What—what happened to Peter—and Simon?" her eyes at once filled with dread. "Are they—were they—?"

"Those things happened over two thousand years ago, my dear," Paul assured her. "They now live in mansions in Heaven beyond human description. So are mansions being prepared for you and yours once you come home to your eternal reward."

"Will I see you again?"

"Of course. The time will come when a thousand years will be as a day, and you will remember these things as if just a short while ago. In the meantime, keep all these things in your heart so that you can relive them whenever you like. And remember, the Spirit of Christ lives within you forever."

Once again, a strong wind came from the west and caused her to shield her eyes. When she opened them, Paul had vanished from sight. She closed them once again and thanked the Lord for all the wondrous things that had happened.

She walked back to the house, resolved that tonight would be the beginning of a journey that would continue unto the rest of her days.

About the Author

I began my so-called career at the age of six, writing dialogue for my stick-figure cartoons. I actually began reading at the age of three, a God-given talent that my parents attested to. Upon entering first grade I refined the technique of expressing words in print, and from there it progressed. By sixth grade I wrote my first novella, a James Bond ripoff called *Enemy Ace*. It was about a WWII German pilot, Fritz Hammer, recruited by the CIA to thwart a negriphile named Blackman. Umm... yeah. Well, guess what? Fritz Hammer appeared in *Tiara* a half century later, and the plot morphed into *The Standard* shortly thereafter. Hmm.

I continued writing through high school, spending one summer writing a 1,000-page epic about the USA turning fascist and starting WWIII. I pulled it in a tad and wrote a second spy novel featuring Fritz Hammer. I lent both of them to two of my teachers and never got them back. At this stage of my life, I am certain that none of us will ever profit from those long-lost treasures.

It really kicked in during my twenties while I was masterminding my punk band, the Spoiler. I wrote a ten-novel series on Richard Mc Cain, a Special Forces superhero in Vietnam. They were action-packed, well-researched classics that never saw the light of day in the pre-Internet days. Mc Cain became the hero of *Bloody Sunday*, an apocalyptic Northern Ireland saga. Again, an awesome piece of work that never went anywhere. Mc Cain became the protagonist of my Christian novel *Abaddon (Destroyer)*, so it wasn't all in vain. I also wrote a half-dozen sci-fi space novels, great action tales that never got published.

When I relocated to Texas, I went through another writing phase which sowed some major fields. I wrote *Hezbollah*, which got published a quarter-century later, as did *The Bat* and *Both Sides Now*. There was also *Tiara*, which was an offshoot of a sci-fi novel I wrote back in NYC. I was really gearing up to make something happen, but that didn't progress until I moved to Missouri.

I ended up going to bed with Publish America, a vanity press rip-off that ended up with some of my best work. They got *Tiara*, then *Wolfsangel*, followed by *Cyclops* and *Penny Flame*. It took four years before I realized they weren't paying me a dime and never would. I decided I had to make a last-ditch effort to make something of my so-called career, and 2013 was the year.

I devoted myself full-time to getting published and put thirty novels on the market. Some were self-published, and many others went to indie lit publishers. I've had over two hundred reviews of my work posted on Amazon. Over eighty percent are five-star reviews. I haven't made any decent money yet, but my readers have made it worthwhile.

What keeps me going? The great, incomparable stories, the awesome characters, and the satisfaction of knowing you are writing things that people will appreciate long after you're gone. I can pick up one of my novels after years of not having read it, and become absorbed by it all over again. I wonder why they never reached the heights that so many farce novels find in Hollywood. I'm not gonna worry about it. My readers know and I know. 'Nuff said.

All I can say is: pick up a JRD novel and see what you think. If you really think it sucks, just write me an e-mail and tell me why. Odds are I'll send you your money back. Or if you're in Kansas City, I'll buy you a beer.

Oh, yeah, and I give all the credit and glory to my Lord Jesus Christ. He put the spirit and the vision inside me. If He didn't like what I was doing, He would've taken it away a half century ago.

And I'm glad He hasn't.

Lightning Source UK Ltd.
Milton Keynes UK
UKHW011158091120
373077UK00001B/202